THE SEVEN QUEENS

.

the seven queens

Sindhi Folktales Retold in English Verse
by
Menka Shivdasani

Translated into Sindhi
by
Barkha Khushalani

BLACK EAGLE BOOKS
Dublin, USA

BLACK EAGLE BOOKS

USA Address:
7464 Wisdom Lane
Dublin, OH 43016

India Address:
E/312, Trident Galaxy, Kalinga Nagar,
Bhubaneswar-751003, Odisha, India

E-mail: info@blackeaglebooks.org
Website: www.blackeaglebooks.org

First International Edition Published by
BLACK EAGLE BOOKS, 2024

The Seven Queens
by Menka Shivdasani

ISBN- 978-1-64560-564-5 (Paperback)

Printed in the United States of America

In memory of

Dr Arjan Shad Mirchandani

(1924 – 2006)

who first introduced me to these tales

.

Other books by Menka Shivdasani

Poetry
Nirvana at Ten Rupees, XAL-Praxis 1990

Stet, Sampark 2000

Safe House, Paperwall Media and Publishing 2015

Frazil (1980 – 2017), Paperwall Media and Publishing

Translations / Bilingual books
Freedom and Fissures, Sahitya Akademi, 1990

Brittle Ice (Mohan Gehani*)*, Copper Coin, 2015

While Sowing Dreams (Mohan Gehani), Black and White Fountain, 2023

Love is the Only Finality: Sindhi Dohiras by Sachal Sarmast (forthcoming, Sahitya Akademi), in collaboration with Mohan Gehani

Books Edited (English)
The BigBridge Anthology of Contemporary Indian Poetry (2024) – (Black Eagle Books, originally published on the American e-zine *www.bigbridge.org* in 2013 and 2015)

If the Roof Leaks, Let it Leak, SPARROW, 2014

Corporate History/Non-Fiction

18 books, co-authored/edited with Raju Kane, including:

Konkan Railway: A Dream Come True (1998)

The Path to Progress (English, translated into Hindi and Marathi) – 2004

Reach for the Stars: The Story of Blue Star Limited, 2018

A Legacy of Learning: Hyderabad (Sind) National Collegiate Board - 7 Decades, 2022

Other books by Barkha Khushalani

Translations

'Slice of Life...' short stories penned by Thakur Chawla in Sindhi translated into English.

'A Passionate Sindhi...' Biography of Harish Dubey written in Sindhi by Holaram Hans translated into English.

"Moon Kheeru Piayanu Chhade Dino", some short stories penned by Sudha Murthy in English from her book *The Day I Stopped Drinking Milk*, translated into Sindhi.

'Sonheri Sukhan', sayings and quotes penned by Dr A. J. Kalam, translated into Sindhi.

Sindhiyat by Tulsidas Pahuja, translated from English into Sindhi Devnagari script.

Borders and Broken Hearts, poems by Gayatri Lakhiani Chawla in English, translated some of these into Sindhi.

Ordinary People, Extraordinary Dreams, short stories penned by Maya Rahi in Sindhi, translated into English.

Poetry

Dadhi thi Vanee, poems in Sindhi for children.

Acknowledgements

Many people contributed to making this book a reality, and I am grateful to each one of them for their support.

- Mohan Gehani, senior Sindhi poet and scholar, for his encouragement, when I was unsure of what I was doing; for ensuring that no factual inaccuracies crept in, and for his close reading and suggestions on both the English originals and the translations;

- Priya Sarrukai Chhabria, poet, translator and editor, for her encouragement in the early days of this project;

- Film-maker Susheel Gajwani, for ensuring no errors crept into the Perso-Arabic pages, and for his enthusiastic response to the work, which included his decision to direct a short film based on the first completed poem on Sasui and Punhoon. I am grateful to all the people associated with this production – Bhagwan Pidwani, who offered the space to shoot it in one of his last acts of generosity before he unexpectedly passed away; Barkha Khushalani for producing the film; cameraman Sanjay Pandit and his team; Amit Aswani, Damini Kane and Bhushan Sanjay Pandit for acting in it;

- Shobha Lalchandani for her logistical support before her untimely demise;

- Barkha Khushalani for her meticulous translations of the English originals and for putting together this collection in all three scripts;

- Anand Lalchandani, Proprietor, Impressions, for typesetting the material and designing the layout;

- Dr Sujata Jadhav, Head - Libraries & Documentation Centre at National Centre for the Performing Arts (NCPA), and Pervin Saket, curator of the Literary section of the Kala Ghoda Arts Festival, for providing performance spaces for these poems, and room for them to breathe; Sukrita Paul Kumar for publishing *Princess of Illusion* in Sahitya Akademi's *Indian Literature.*

- Raju Kane and Damini Kane, my family members, for being the first readers and for their insightful comments;

- Anju Makhija, who first got me thinking about reclaiming the Sindhi heritage when she asked, back in the 1990s, if I would be interested in working with her on translations of Sindhi Partition poetry;

- And a special thank you to Satya Pattanaik of the USA-based Black Eagle Books, for so readily agreeing to publish this work.

Contents

Foreword

The Bhimbetka caves near Bhopal are a world heritage site. The ceilings have paintings going back to the Neolithic age. On a visit to these caves, I wondered what must have impelled the caveman to make colour from flowers, a brush from the stem of a tree and a scaffolding-type contraption to paint animals that were being hunted by Man. After some reflection, I thought that some people have a very strong desire to imitate and share their experiences, and they become restless until they find release. Their urge to express themselves is very strong and they would endure any exertion to give expression to their experience and emotion. Fortunately, this urge has not remained limited to the Stone Age man. It continues today and is the foundation of all arts.The journey of Man from the Cave to the threshold of the interstellar journey is fascinating indeed.

For a child, learning a language in itself is a process of imitation. Children have innocence, fertile imagination and the curiosity to play and explore their surroundings. When these combine with the quest of 'What', 'Why', and 'How' simultaneously, it leads to discoveries, inventions, and explorations, both within and without. In fact, these three words have propelled all that we call 'Progress'. Without these key words, progress would not be possible. In the process of imitation and exploration, innocence and curiosity, stories are born. For a child in his innocence and imagination, birds, bees and rivers speak. 'Magic' becomes real. Fairy tales take wings, and the world of wonder awakens.

As the child moves into youth, Love becomes an overpowering emotion. At that time love stories become more interesting. As love has many hues and is enduring, there are many stories and they become folktales. These folktales remain the ideal for youth for a very long time. In fact, tales are like floating clouds in the sky. Sometimes, some part is detached and connected to other parts, and sometimes, an interpolation in the tale intervenes and settles in it for all time. This way, we have many versions of the same tale at different times and places. This phenomenon of fairy tales and folktales is common all over the world and is true for every time, place, and society which has tales of love. Simultaneously, religion holds an important place for a durable moral and social structure in society. In fact, since time immemorial, it has addressed the fundamental insecurity built into the human psyche.

Sind has its tales as well, and though some are not located in Sind, they have been part of the Sindhi folk tradition for a long time. It is said that it was during the Soomra period that these tales became popular in Sind. Before the Partition of the country, Dr. Hotchand Gurbuxani did extensive research on Shah Latif, and as a part of that research, he dwelt at length on the tales immortalised by the great poet. Shah Latif is often referred to as the soul of Sindhi culture. His verses have become part of common conversation in rural Sind. After 1947, Dr. Nabi Khan Baloch collected various versions of folktales in more than 40 volumes. Prof Ram Panjwani also documented these tales with some historical footnotes after Partition. Prof. Pritam Varyani compiled a small book in Sindhi (which this writer later translated into English.)

Many songs also reference these tales, and sometimes *bhagats*[1] devoted their entire performances to these stories. In the Sufi tradition of Sindhi culture, these tales have been invested with otherworldly and mystical meaning, and many critics have seen

---

[1] *Bhagat is a Sindhi folk art that incorporates song, dance, drama and story.*

them through that prism. In a traditional way, these tales are moral and spiritual instructions.

The present poems by Menka Shivdasani based on folktales, translated into Sindhi by Barkha Khushalani, show the main characters of these stories simply as human beings with natural emotions, and they are significantly rendered through two main characters. Menka's efforts are more important in light of the fact that many of our new generations, not being educated in Sindhi, are unaware of their rich heritage. In a way, she built a bridge to enable them to connect with their roots and rich heritage. In this context, her work assumes great significance.

She is a seasoned poet in her own right, and I will not add anything to that aspect of her poetry as it speaks for itself. Her treatment of the folktale narration only through two main characters catches the essence of the story in a remarkable manner. By her deft handling, she imparts immortality to the characters, and they continue to be united for all time, signifying an unending bond of love. A few examples of her poetic flight will not be out of place. Her opening lines in the folktale of Leela-Chanesar, *Diamonds and Coal*, depict the process of creation – nature in action itself.

"*What is coal*
and what is diamond
is for the earth to decide
in the stillness of its core,
when heat and light coalesce silently
or in a rumbling heaving roar.
I sank into the depths and confused
the difference between the two..."

In the tale of Sohini-Mehar, the beauty of arresting expression is self-evident. *"Mud and clay for me are the beginning/ the source of all that is good and true…"* In the tale of Moomal-Rano, she unravels the ultimate mystery of life when she says, *"But tell me, love/ in this game of chess/ did either one of us win?"*

I have given these examples to whet the reader's appetite and indicate the gamut of emotional experiences that lie open before you to savour.

I congratulate Menka Shivdasani for accomplishing such a wondrous feat.

MOHAN GEHANI
June 2024
Bhopal

Author's Note

The first time I encountered Sindhi folktales was when I was in my thirties, working on translations of Sindhi Partition poetry. It was the noted poet Dr Arjan Shad who introduced me to them; strangely, though folktales are usually a part of every child's lexicon while growing up, these stories lay buried in the debris of Partition, lost to new generations who had never known the homeland of their elders. Dr. Shad pointed out that each of these stories represented key aspects of human nature – for instance, Marui was a symbol of Patriotism, Noori of Humility.

Some years later, in 2011, I read these stories in more detail. Prof. Pritam Varyani, who was in his eighties when I met him at the Indian Institute of Sindhology in Adipur, had made it his life's mission to recover these tales, mining them from remote regions that are still a stronghold of these legends. When we spoke, Prof. Varyani pointed out that while folktales were an integral part of human culture and communication in rural landscapes, they were increasingly being silenced in a rapidly urbanising world. As a post-Partition child born and brought up in Bombay (now Mumbai), they certainly belonged nowhere in my life.

Fortunately for me and for others who wanted to know more, Prof. Varyani wrote a book on the subject, committing these oral tales to the printed page. The book, *Sindhi Folk Tales,* published by the Indian Institute of Sindhology, first appeared in 2006, in the Perso-Arabic script that had few readers in post-Partition India. In 2008, he republished it in the Sindhi Devanagari script, and then in 2009, Mohan Gehani translated the work into English. This version, also published by the same organisation, has been invaluable; my now dog-eared copy has accompanied me on many travels where I hoped I would have the space and mind space to work on my own retelling.

The folktales of Sind are numerous and have many fantastical elements. Lal Shahbaz, born Hazrat Sayad Usman Shah Marwandi in Afghanistan in A.H. 538, dropped his *kishta,* or begging bowl, into the water, and it became a boat. When he and his friends were attacked by a baker's wife who claimed – falsely – that one of their party, Sheikh Farid Shakar Ganj, had tried to outrage her, the saint changed one of his friends into a deer and another into a lion. He then transformed himself into a peregrine falcon, swooped down, and took poor Sheikh Farid to a place of safety, thus earning the moniker the Red Peregrine Falcon of the Indus Valley. When he died, it is believed that streams of molasses, sugar and milk spurted from the walls of his tomb, but when rich and poor rushed greedily to relish these, the disgusted saint made the streams turn dry. All that remains of them, writes C A Kincaid, author of *Folk Tales of Sind and Guzarat,* first published by The Daily Gazette Press Ltd (Karachi, 1925), "is a group of stones that look exactly like petrified sugar molasses and milk. These the guardians of the shrine shew to wondering pilgrims as proof positive of the legend's truth."

As M. de P. Webb wrote (London, December 16, 1924) in the Foreword to C. A. Kincaid's book: "The stories which have been passed on from generation to generation are, like the legends of the West, to some extent, mythical, but no doubt based on actual incidents in the past, which, in the repeated telling, have been added to and embroidered in a way calculated to impress the minds of the simple folk who heard them; and thus their remembrance and transmission to later generations has been assured."

Such myths surround the classical poet, Shah Abdul Latif, as well. Latif, who was born in 1668, is said to have turned himself into a pigeon so that he could coo to the beautiful Moghul girl he loved when her father, Mirza Beg, ordered him off the premises. Mirza Beg was not fooled and threatened to set his falcons upon him.

The legend of Uderolal makes for another riveting tale. Born in Nassarpur to the family of Rattan Rao Luhana to save Hindus from the despotic governor of Thatta, Marak, Uderolal is said to have transformed from infant to youth to old man in an instant and risen from the river with thousands of soldiers, horsemen, elephants, and chariots. In Sanskrit, 'Udero' means 'the one who has sprung from the waters', and it is believed the child was an incarnation of Lord Varuna. Uderolal's cradle kept swinging on its own – like the waves of the Sindhu (Indus) river, as one commentator, Shewak Nandwani, described it. Uderolal, therefore, also became known as 'Jhulelal' – the swinging child[2] – the popular appellation by which the Ishtadeva is known to Sindhi Hindus in India today.

There are other tales. In his book, Prof. Varyani has shared stories of Koel and Deepchand, lovers from different communities who surmounted many odds to be together. The story of brave Dodo and Abro is based on historical characters and speaks of the courage of Sindhi and Kutchi rulers in a fierce succession battle. And there is Moriro, the lame but clever Boatman, who captures the crocodile who has killed his six brothers. In the end, I chose to focus on the Seven Queens (*Sat Surmiyoon*) that Shah Latif brought to life in his iconic *Shah Jo Risalo*.

I must admit that, to my untrained eye and sceptical ear, these stories, at first glance, seemed absurd. My immediate impression was that people kept falling in love with those they had never met simply because they had heard about how beautiful they were. To make it worse, they also seemed to keep fainting because of this unrequited love, sometimes dropping dead when they did so! There had to be more to these stories, and I decided I had to find out.

---

[2] *https://www.jhulelal.com/completestory.htm, Retrieved May 2024*

During this journey, which ended up taking several years, I discovered many books on Sind, detailing its landscapes and legends; the more I read, the less I knew, and the greater the enthusiasm to tread these long-forgotten paths. As I read the stories, logic and reason became stumbling blocks, but far in the distance, there were new realities that I – an atheist – began to recognise. The spiritual truths these allegories conveyed were universal and had nothing to do with the organised religion that so taints our lives in the divided world we live in today. There is divinity in all of us, as the Sufi saints say, and these connections with our deepest selves resonate as much in modern times as they did 5,000 and more years ago. The only way to do this project, I found, was to suspend all disbelief and listen.

Over time, what began to appeal to me the most about these folktales was the fact that the women had agency – they went after whatever they wanted rather than waiting like wilted roses for life to happen to them. If Sasui wanted to meet her lover Punhoon, she was willing to traverse mountains; Sohini swam into a stormy swollen river for Mehar; Moomal disguised herself as a rich merchant to win back Rano's love. I realised that if the stories themselves seemed fantastic, the human qualities they embodied certainly continued to exist, and there was a great deal here that my own feminist sensibilities could respond to.

As Dr Fahmida Hussain writes in her insightful book, *Image of 'Woman' in the Poetry of Shah Abdul Latif:* "The female characters of Shah's era had all the signs of helplessness and slavery but through his poetry, along with showing the entire social setup, Shah wanted people to see another image of a woman, a different and novel image!" Dr Hussain further points out that Latif wanted to show that women had unique qualities; "she is more intense than a man in patriotism, height of character, sacrifice and determination; she has been made victim of different complexes, and in spite of her poverty she has superior human qualities."[3].

Retelling these tales in my own poetic compositions in English meant that I also needed to learn more about the history, geography, and minutiae of daily life in ancient Sind. I found myself devouring every book on the subject that I could lay my hands on – some of them with the help of supportive friends like Barkha Khushalani and Saaz Aggarwal. Among these were H.T. Lambrick's *Sind: A General Introduction*, first published in 1964 by the Sindhi Adabi Board in Sindh; *The Sindh Story: A Great Account on Sindh* by Dada Kewalram Ratanmal Malkani, first published in 1984 and *Six Thousand Years of History of Irrigation in Sindh* by M.H. Panhwar, compiled by Umer Soomro in October 2011, to name just three. H.T. Sorley's 1940 translation of the *Shah Jo Risalo* became an invaluable reference point[4]. During this process, I realised more than four years had passed before I wrote a single line!

In the end, I decided to get on with the work and explore questions as they arose. Each story brought a new challenge. Before soap was invented, what did *dhobis* use to wash clothes? Five thousand years ago, how did a potter's wheel function? Could camels run as fast as horses? What shrubs, if any, grew in the burning landscapes of the Thar? Beyond the seemingly tiny details, there were other questions. How could I navigate the vast timelines of these stories and connect them to contemporary times? Could these tales even be relevant today in our crazy, chaotic world?

[3.] Hussain, Dr Fahmida and Memon, Dr Amjad Siraj (tr.), Image of 'Woman' in the Poetry of Shah Abdul Latif, University of Karachi, 2011

[4.] Sorley, H.T., Shah Abdul Latif Of Bhit: His Poetry, Life And Times, *A Study of Literary, Social and Economic Conditions in Eighteenth Century Sind,* Oxford University Press, London, 1940

There is much in these stories that our modern mindsets will find hard to accept. But having struggled with this myself, I believe that these folktales are timeless for a reason; they hold a mirror to the one thing that has not changed over the centuries – human nature. These are stories of love and lust, greed and humility, patriotism and deceit, weakness and strength of character – everything that defines our lives as individuals and as communities. That's why I believe they continue to be relevant.

They are also an integral part of the rich legacy of Sindhi culture that we began to lose when the Partition of the Indian sub-continent took place. Few Sindhis of my generation in India have grown up listening to these stories. For that reason alone, I believe they deserve to be resurrected.

While working on this project, Mohan Gehani's English translations gave me many insights into these stories, and his continued support kept me going. It was Gayatri Lakhiani Chawla's *Borders and Broken Hearts*, a trilingual collection for which I had written the Foreword, that made me first think of taking this work into another dimension. Who better to approach than Barkha Khushalani, who had grown up with these tales and who could feel them in her bones? In this journey, I could not have asked for better collaborators and I am grateful to them for their support.

MENKA SHIVDASANI
June 2024

Translator's Note

In December 2021, I read *Call of the Mountains*, a unique dialogue between two eternal lovers, Sasui and Punhoon, written by Menka Shivdasani in English. I was fascinated by this novel idea of a dialogue between the characters of Shah Abdul Latif's *Sat Surmiyoon* and was instantly transported to Bhambhor and Kech Makran. That is the magic of Menka's writings.

When she approached me to transcreate all the seven stories of Shah Abdul Latif into Sindhi, I was touched by her trust in me and confidence in my work. Translation enables effective communication between people around the world and builds bridges of global culture. It serves as a protector of a language and cultural heritage.

Shah Abdul Latif has played a very big role in my life because my mother, Paru Chawla, was a die-hard fan of Shah Sahib's mystic poetry. I have grown up to the music of his 'kalaams', which mummy would sing practically every day. She knew hundreds of couplets from *Shah jo Risalo* and would quote them in every situation in life to express her feelings and educate us about their richness. Hence, I was more than happy to take up this responsibility without even blinking my eyes as I, too, am a fan of the mystical poetry of Shah Abdul Latif.

Menka's concept and imagination while writing the dialogues between the characters of all seven stories are remarkable. The icing on the cake was that at every stage, I was guided by my favourite writer and a truly humble person, Mr Mohan Gehani, who very patiently explained the nuances of the Sindhi language to me. I would also like to thank film-maker Susheel Gajwani for encouraging me to give my best. I missed my beloved sister, Shobha Lalchandani, every moment while working on this project.

Working with Mohan Gehani and Menka Shivdasani, two talented people, was like a bonanza offer for me, and I am sure that through Menka's writings in English, Sindhis all over the world will learn about the greatness of Shah Abdul Latif.

Thank you, Menka, for giving me this opportunity to do my bit towards Sindhi language and poetry.

BARKHA KHUSHALANI
June 2024

The Sindhu Roars

In the arid spaces of the heart
deep beneath sand dunes and the rocks,
ghost oceans shiver in the dark,
bringing rivers gushing out
through cracks in hardened sand.

And where the hardened sand
crumbles into cracks
the water rushes, swallows all the land.

In this cradle of civilisation rocked by its rulers –
Habbaris and Soomras, Sammas and Arghuns,
mendicants and monarchs of the Kalhora clan –
the grandeur and ruins of the Mughal court –
legends lived on the old Kumbar Road,
in the melodies of Munchar Lake birds.
And as the *karvaans* of Kandahar
brought stories and silks to Sind,
in the distance, the Sarasvati
buried its head in the sand.

The Sindhu still roars,
a conch shell against the ear.
Its waters turn,
drowning the *palla*, breaking

the banks, sweeping away
the hutments of the mind.
Mudflats choke, and trees collapse.
The thorn bush on the banks of the Indus
stands alone with no memory of the flood.
The water simmers in the turgid land,
waiting to break ashore.
Like rivers, dammed, uncertain,
we nose our way to newer paths,
past rocks and rubble,
the silt of memory.

Into these turbid waters, I throw my *kishta*
under Lal Shahbaz's watchful eye,
hope it will transform into an argosy.

And we come together like grains of sand in the restless wind,
blown apart in an instant in the howling storm.
Far on the horizon, the lone leafless shrub
sways to the sighs of ancient queens.

Listen – for they sing to you.
their broken tunes still sweet in the desert wind.

Call of the Mountains

Sasui, within yourself you bear
what you are seeking so.
No one ever found anything
by walking here and there...

Call of the Mountains

Sasui

Vendor of musk, we must meet again.
The scent of my longing is like wine.

In the haze of the wilderness,
as mountains stretch,
I see the shimmer
of caravans burning
in the distance.
Punhoon, my prince,
your fragrance rides the sun,
caresses my blistered feet.
For a moment, a river flows
through my parched mind.
This moment is divine,
but it will pass.

Vendor of musk, we must meet again.
The scent of my longing is like wine.

I, Sasui, who has harnessed the moon,
felt the Bambrah in my bones,
I know the rough edges
of wicker on my skin.
I was a baby when they set me afloat
to meet my fate in distant lands.
Though my ageing parents
Naoon and Mandhur,

loved me,
they sent me away
when the pundit
gazed into my newborn eyes
and drew my future
in the sand.
'She will marry a Muslim,'
he said, and their faith
would not allow it!

So I learned to speak
with the stars
that guided my path,
and they brought you,
my love, to me.
I seek you now, Punhoon,
through stone-hearted cliffs.
I gasp in this shrinking air
but no mountain or desert will defeat me.

Vendor of musk, we must meet again.
The scent of my longing is like wine.

Punhoon
My love,
I searched so hard for you.
from the lonely peaks of Balochistan,
where they knew me
as Prince of Kech Makran,
son of Aari Jaam,
but for me, this was not enough.

I traversed through ridges,
valleys and peaks,
on the road to Thatta
selling ribbons and musk.
Tales of your beauty were my compass
and this trader's garb
became my second skin.
I had no jewels upon me then;
there was just one I needed,
and that was you,
whom I found,
and lost.

I had heard of Mohammed,
the washerman,
chief of his tribe at Bhambor
how you floated up
by the riverbank,
unscathed by currents,
protected by God.
I had heard of his kindness,
how he became the only
father you knew.
The days spun like cotton
and the spinning wheel
spun towards me;
my heart was caught
in the silken
threads of love.

Your face is the moon, your heart my guiding star,
Sasui, my love, open the heavens for me.

Sasui

Punhoon, my Prince,
I hear you,
like the breeze
gentle upon my ears.
But above me
is an unrelenting sky;
on the ground,
my toes begin to bleed.
I see you smile
on the mountain top;
I step forward
and you are gone.
There's a *karvaan*
in the distance;
I wish I could be
a grain of sand
in a camel's eye,
which would take me
closer to you.

How delightful it was
when your caravan arrived
in what seems like a lifetime ago!
Happiness was a bottle
of rare perfume –
such wonders
that I had never seen!
Necklaces of shell,
bangles of Baloch,
so delicate,
in rainbow shades.
But it was you

who brought the most joy.
These dizzying wares paled
in your presence.
How heavenly it was
to be with you.
How much you gave up
with such grace!

Vendor of musk, we must meet again.
The scent of my longing is like wine.

Punhoon
Sasui, my love,
is that your voice in my dreams?
I hear you in a haze
but where are you?
How happy I was
in those *dhobi ghats*,
knowing I would
come home to your smile!
The tribal chief turned me
into a washerman,
testing my love
and my skill at clothes.
'He's not from our caste!'
Mohammed said,
and I had to prove him wrong.
You were so clever, Sasui.
Unused to the labour,
I tore the garments,
but no one complained.
A gold coin tucked
into each damaged dress

was a small price to pay
for our love.
And what did it matter
if a few clothes were ripped,
when our hearts
were stitched together!

The promise that Mohammed extracted
to stay in Bhambhor
was easy enough for me.
I could not return to my king, anyway,
for my queen was here in these *ghats*.
Our laughter, like lather,
bubbled over, and the days
turned to froth in our hands.
We were happy, Sasui,
until my brothers arrived.
You gave them so much love.
But they battered us
on the *dhobi ghat*,
wrung us out
like faded cloth,
tore the seams of our lives.
Chunro, Hotu, Notu –
what have you done!
You must believe me, Sasui.
The night they dragged me away
intoxicated on camelback,
I had not drunk so much;
there was toxic wine in my glass,
and they knew it well.

Your face is the moon, your heart my guiding star,
Sasui, my love, open the heavens for me.

Sasui

My heart is in pieces,
like the clay *kadas* I wore,
and this wasteland does not end.
The scent of the Sarasvati
lies deep within its bones.
But at night the thirsty foxes hunt,
and nature itself is the enemy –
the wind that took your footprints away;
the sun, which refuses to set,
the sky that burns and snuffs
the cool air out,
the moon that casts dark shadows
in these haunted hills.
Bears, baboons and wolves
rear up to block my path.
But as long as life,
like a migrant traveller,
shuffles beneath my skin,
I must keep moving, Punhoon;
I must see your face
or my thirst will not be quenched.

For a minute, hope sprang
at the Pubba mountain,
where water gushed
from a rocky mound
and your face rippled
back at me and smiled;
I cupped my palms in you;
your strength flowed
into my face,
and the spring returned

to my step in the lonely expanse.
I made it to Mabuhur,
where a hut on a hillock rose,
and my heart surged again
on the jagged path
that another human had crossed.
But Punhoon, this shepherd
had an ugly smile,
and I was not his sheep.
I asked for water,
and when he turned his back,
I prayed, Punhoon,
to save me from his grasping hands
and the hillock broke into two;
I fell into its womb.

Vendor of musk, I will meet you again.
We shall be one with the Divine.

Punhoon

The ground has cracked
beneath my feet.
Your absence is sharp
against my throat.
Sasui, I must find you,
I must return;
my brothers
must let me go.
The king, my father,
wanted me back
but he will not see me die.
So I ask if I can bring you here
to call Kech Makran your own.

The canyons are calling,
and I will leave
on the fastest camel I can find.
My brothers – betrayers –
join me; they dare not
disobey Aari Jam.
In the burning
landscape of my being,
Sasui, you stand sturdy
as the *khabar* tree.

But what is that at the Mabuhur?
Oh, Shepherd, which saint's
fresh grave lies here?
And what is this silken fragment
that peeps up from the ground?
Surely I have seen it in Bhambor!
It is a garment that Sasui wore.
But how is it here
trapped in this terrain?
Shepherd, tell me the story,
and I will tell you mine.

Sasui, are you there?
This silence is more
than I can bear.

And the earth moves,
the ridges crumble,
I fall feet first into the crack.
The heavens open up
in the ground beneath
the Shepherd's feet

The moon shines bright
on shifting rock.
I hear you now, Sasui,
as I hear myself.

Punhoon, you have come to me; I will no longer pine.
For we are, at last, One in the Divine.

जबलनि जी पुकार

ससुई

पुन्हूं मुश्क जो सौदागार आहीं,
न न मां भायां को जादूगर आहीं,

तुंहिंजीअ सिक जे नशे आ तरिसायो,
दूरि बयाबान जी धुंधि में,
जबलनि जे झुंड में,
मां थी डिसां रोशन कारवां,
पून्हूं मुंहिंजा राजकुमार,
तुंहिंजी मोहींदड़ महक,
सिज खे छुही,
मुंहिंजे फटियल पेरनि
खे चुमियो आहे,
हिक खिन लाए
मुंहिंजे सुकायल मन में,
हिक नदी कल-कल वहे थी,
इहो पलु इलाही आहे,
पर तकिड़ो गुज़िरी वेंदो,
मुश्क जा जादूगर सौदागर,

ब्रिहर मिलंदासीं,
तुंहिंजीअ सिक जे नशे आ तरिसायो.

मां ससुई आहियां, जहिं चंड जी
ताक़त खे क़ाबू कयो,

पर नंढिपिण में बांबिड़ा
पाईंदे सूर खे न विसारियो,
मां त नओं ज़ावलु ब़ारु हुयसि,
जड़िहं हुननि संदूक में बंदि
करे नदीअ में फिटो कयो,
दलूग़इ दूरि ब़ीअ धरितीअ ड़ांहं,
लेखु विधाता जो कीअं चुकायां?
मुंहिंजा माता पिता
नाओं ऐं मांधुर
मूंखे प्यारु कंदा हुआ,
पर मूंखे पाण खां
परे मोकिलियाउनि
पंडित जी अग़कथी जा
मुंहिंजे कोमल अखियुनि मां
ज़ाहिरु थी
हीअ मुसलमान सां शादी कंदी
हुन चयो ऐं मुंहिंजनि
माइटनि जो धर्मु ड़िकियो
अड़े! ईअं न थे!
त मां तारनि सां
ग़ाल्हियूं करण लग़सि,
सितारा मुंहिंजा रहिनुमा थिया
मूंखे तो ड़ांहुं छिर्कींदा आया,
हाणि मां तोखे पुन्हूं पत्थर दिलि
टकिरियुनि में ग़ोल्हियां थी,
भलि रिण जी रेत मूं खे
घुटे पर को बि

बरभंगु मूंखे हाराए न सघंदो
पुन्हूं
मुंहिंजा प्यारा!
मुश्क जो जादूगर सौदागर
बिहर मिलदांसीं,
तुंहिंजीअ सिक जे नशे आ तरिसायो!

पुन्हूं

मुंहिजी प्यारी,
मूं तुंहिंजी तलाश हरि हंद कई,
बलोचिस्तान जे उब्राणिकी
जबल चोट तां
जिति मूंखे सभि
केच मकरान जो राजकुमार,
आरी ज़ाम जो पुटु करे
सुञाणीनि,
पर मुंहिंजो वजूदु तूं आहीं,
मां ब्रना, माथारी चोट सभि
आर–पार लघें आयुसि
थटे जी राह ड्रांहु,
खथूरी ऐं रिबीनूं विकिरंदे,
तुंहिंजीअ सूंहं जी वखाण
हुई मुंहिंजो रहिबरु
ऐं हीउ वापारीअ जो वेसु
बणियो मुंहिंजे जिस्म जो हिसो,
न हुआ मूंखे के ज़ेवर,
मूंखे ग़ोल्हा हुई हिक रत्न जी,

जा हुईअं तूं,
जिहिं खे मूं पाए विआयो,
मूं मोहमद धोबीअ जो नालो बुधो हो,
जो भंभोर में क़बीले जो सरदारु हो,
कीअं तूं सही सलामत
नदीअ जे तेज़ वहिकरे खां बचीयं,
खुदा बणियो तुंहिंजो निगहबानु,
धोबीअ तुंहिंजे पिता,
जो रुप धारण कयो,
ड़ींहं कपह जीआं कतिबा विया,
ऐं चरिखो मूं तरफ़ वधंदो आयो,
मुंहिंजी दिलि तुंहिंजे प्रेम जे कचन
धागुनि में अटिकी
तुंहिंजो चंड जहिड़ो चहिरो
आ मुंहिंजो रहिबरु सितारो,
ससुई मुंहिंजी प्यारी,
सुर्ग रूपी आकाश खोलि
त मां तो में समाइजी वञा.

ससुई
पुन्हूं मुंहिंजा राजकुमार,
मां तोखे बुधां थी,
उन्हीअ रिण जी हीर
जीआं जा हलिके सां कन
ते सुणाए थी,
पर मुंहिंजे मथां,
आ हीउ कठोर आस्मानु,

ऐं ज़मीन ते पेरनि
मां रतु ज़ारु ज़ारु वहे,
मूं तोखे मुरकंदो डिठो,
मां जबल जी चोट तां,
अगि॒ते वधियसि
ऐं तूं लापता थी विऐं,
दूरि हिकु कारिवां डि॒सां थी,
काशि मां उठ जे अख में
वारीअ जो कणो हुजां,
जेको तोखे मुंहिजे क॒रीबु आणे,
तुंहिंजा कारवां डि॒सी,
मां ख़ुशीअ विचां गदि॒ गदि॒,
ज॒णु के जन्म गुज़िरी विया तोखे डि॒ठे!
ज॒णु ख़ुशी हिक अनोखे इतर
जी बोतल में बंदि॒,
अहिड़ा अजूबा मूं न डि॒ठा न बुधा!
सिपुनि जूं माल्हाऊं,
बलोच जा चूड़ा,
कोमल ऐं नाज़ुक,
सतरंगी रंगनि में जड़ियल,
पर मूंखे तालि तुंहिंजी,
मुंहिंजी ख़ुशी सिर्फ़ तूं,
तुंहिंजे साम्हूं सभि हीरा
जवाहर असुलु फिका,
तो सां मिलणु को
सुर्ग जो सैर हो,
मुंहिंजे लाए तो सवें

त्याग कया खिलंदे खिलंदे!
मुश्क जा जादूगर सौदागर,
ब्रिहर मिलंदासीं,
तुंहिंजीअ सिक जे नशे आ तरिसायो!

पुन्हूं

ससुई मुंहिंजी प्यारी,
छा मुंहिंजे सुपननि में,
तुंहिंजो आवाजु आहे?
कननि ते को धुंधिलो परलाउ,
पर तूं किथे आहीं?
धोबी घाटनि में
मां केड्रो न ख़ुशि हुयिसु,
इन्तज़ारु हूंदो हो घर पहुची
तुंहिंजो खिलमुख चहिरो पसां!
क़बीले जे सरदारु मूं खे
धोबी ठाहे छड्रियो,
मुंहिंजे नींहं खे परखण लाए,
ऐं कपिड़ा धुअण जे हुनर तपासण लाए,
हीउ असांजे ज़ाति जो नाहे,
मोहम्मद चयो,
मूंखे हुन खे ग़लत
साबिति करणो हुओ,
ससुई, तूं केड्री त सियाणी हुईयं,
मूंखे त धुअण जी ज़ाण न हुई,
मां त कपड़ा फाड़ींदो रहियुसि,
पर कहिं बि शिकायत न कई,

हरि फाटल कपिड़े में तो
हिकु सोनो सिको लिकायो,
असांजे प्यार लाए सोनु त
नंढी कीमत हुई,
के कपिड़ा उखिड़ियां
त का वड़ी ग़ुल्हि नाहे,
पर असांजी प्रीति जा टोपा पुख़्ता थिया!
मोहम्मद सां मूं वादो कयो,
त मां भंभोर में ई रहंदुसि,
उते रहणु मुंहिंजे लाए सवलो हुओ,
हूअं बि पंहिंजे राज़ु वञी न सघां हा,
मुंहिंजी दिलि जी राणी त
हिते घाटनि में हुई,
असांजा टह टह कंदा टहिक,
मुलायम गजीअ, जीआं वधंदा रहिया,
ऐं ड़ींहं खिलंदे गुज़िरी विया,
ससुई असां ख़ुशीअ में रुधल ऐं बेफ़िक्र
जेसि तांई मुंहिंजा भाउर आया,
तो हुननि खे केड़ो न प्यारु ड़िनो,
पर हुननि असां सां ज़्यादती कई,
धोब्री घाटनि ते कहिं पुराणे
कपिड़े जीआं निपूड़ियो,
असांजे जीवन जी तंदु टुटी,
चुनरा, होतू, नोतू......
तव्हां हीउ छा कयो?
ससुई मूं ते यक़ीन करि
जड़िहं उन्हीअ राति हू

मूंखे नशे में उठ ते चाढ़े
खणी विया,
मूं शराबु कान्ह पीतो हो,
मुंहिंजे पियाले में नशीली मदिरा हुई
जेका हुननि खे ख़बर हुई,
तुंहिंजो चंड जहिड़ो चहिरो
आ मुंहिंजो रहिबरु सितारो,
ससुई मुंहिंजी प्यारी,
सुर्ग रूपी आकाशि खोलि,
त मां तो में समाइजी वञा.

ससुई
मुंहिंजी दिलि टुकिरा टुकिरा थी आहे,
चीकी मिटीअ जे चूड़े जीआं,
असांजी पीड़ा बेअंत आहे.
सरस्वती नदीअ जी खुशिबूइ,
हड़-हड़ में समायल,
पर कारी राति में लूमड़ शिकारु कनि,
ऐं कुदिरत पाण दुश्मन थिए,
हवा जहिं तुंहिंजे पेरनि जा,
निशान डाहे छड़िया,
ऐं सिजु त न लहण जे ज़िद ते आ,
ब्रंदड़ आकाशु थधी हवा सुणिके,
चंड जा कारा पाछा पवनि,
हिननि गिरहणु लगुल टकिरियूनि ते,
रिछ, बांदर, बघड़
सभि मुंहिंजो रस्तो रोकीनि,

पर जेसीं जानि आहे,
लड़ियल मुसाफ़िर जे,
चोले में,
मूंखे अग्रिते हलणो आ, पुन्हूं
जेसी तांई मां तोखे न ड्रिसां,
मुंहिंजी उञ न मिटंदी.
हिक पल लाए उमेद जाग्री;
पबे जबल जी चोट ते,
जितां पाणी ज़ोर सां
वहियो हिक टकिराइते दड़ मां,
तुंहिंजो सुहिणो चिहरो छलिकियो,
मूं ड्रांहुं मुरिकियो,
मूं तुंहिंजो चिहरो हथनि
में भरियो,
तुंहिंजी रूहानी ताक़त
तेज़ीअ सां मुंहिंजे चिहरे में उथी,
चशिमो उछिली मोटी
मुंहिंजे पेरनि ते उब्राणिकी वारीअ विचि,
मां धीरे धीरे मबुहर पहुतसि,
जिते हिक टकिरीअ मां नंढी झूंपिड़ी,
नज़र आई,
ऐं दिलि में वरी उमंग जाग्री,
नोकीली दग्र ते हिकु
ब्रियो माणिहू ईंदो ड्रिठो,
पर पुन्हूं हीउ रेढारू,
हिन जी नज़र त ख़राब आ,
मां त हिन जी रिढ नाहियां,

मूं हुन खां पाणी घुरियो,
ऐं जड़िहं हूउ वरियो,
मूं भगि़वान खे यादि कयो, पुन्हूं,
मूं अर्जु कयो त मूं खे हुन खां बचाए,
ऐं टकिरी बि़नि हिसनि में टुटी,
मां, मां धरतीअ जे गर्भ में
समाइजी वियसि,
मुश्क जा जादूगर, सौदागर,
बि़हर मिलंदासी,
असीं अलह सां गु़डिजी हिकु थींदासी.

पुन्हूं

ज़मीन चीरजी पेई आहे,
मुंहिंजे पेरनि हेठां,
तुंहिंजीअ ग़ैरहाजुरीअ
मूंखे मारे छडि़यो,
ससुई! मां तो खे लोचे लहां.
मां मोटी ईंदुसि,
मुंहिंजा भाउर
उमेद त मूंखे वञण ड़ीदां,
राजा मुंहिंजे पिता,
चाहियो त मां हुन वटि वञा,
पर हूउ मूंखे मरंदो,
सही न सघंदो,
त मां पुछां थो त मां तोखे
हिते वठी अचां,
जीअं केच मकरान खे,

तूं पंहिंजो समुझी.
वीरानो सड़े रहियो आहे,
ऐं मां वञा थो,
सभिनी खां तकिड़े उठ ग़ोल्हे,
मुंहिंजा भाउर टेई दग़ाबाज़,
छा मूं सां थींदा...
हू आरी ज़ाम खे न मञण जी,
जुरिअत न कंदा,
मुंहिंजे मन जे गर्म मंजर में
ससुई तूं खबड़ वण,
जीआं मज़िबूति बीठी आहीं,
पर हूउ मबुहुर में छा आहे?
ओ रेढार, हीअ कहिड़े संत,
जी क़बर आ? ताज़ी ऐं मिटी आली!
हीउ रेशमी कपिड़े जो टुकुरु,
जेको ज़मीन तां नज़र थो अचे ?
कहिंजो आ? मूं त पक भंभोर में,
ड़िठो आ,
हीउ त ससुई जो रओ आ,
पर हिति कीअं पहुतो?
रेढार, मूंखे पंहिंजी कहाणी बुधाए
ऐं मां तोखे पंहिंजी
दास्तान बुधाईंदुसि,
ससुई, तूं हिति आहीं छा?
हीउ सनाटो मां,
सही न सघंदुसि
ज़मीन ज़ोर सां धुड़ी,

ब॒ना भुरण लग॒ा,
मां चीर मां पेरनि सां अंदर किरियुसि,
मथे सुर्ग खुलण जा आसार,
हेठ ज़मीन में रेढार जा पेर,
आस्मान में चंड॒ु चिमिकियो
हलंदड़ वारीअ विचि,
हा ससुई, हाणे मां तो खे
बुधां थो,
पाण खे बि बुधां थो

*पुन्हूं तूं मूं वटि आयो आहीं, हाणि मां न सिकंदसि
छाकाण त असां ब॒ुई अलाह सां हिकु थिया आहियूं!*

جبلن جي پُڪار

سسُئي

پُنهون مُشڪ جو سوداگر آهين،

نَ نَ مان پايان ڪو جادوگر آهين،

تنهنجيءَ سِڪ جي نشي آ ترسِيو،

دُور بيابان جي ڏنڊ ۾،

مان تي ڏسان روشن ڪاروان،

پنهون منهنجا راجڪمار،

تنهنجي موهيندڙ مهڪ،

سج ڪي چُهي،

منهنجي قتيل پيرن،

ڪي چميو آهي.

هڪ ڪِن لاءِ،

منهنجي سُڪايل من ۾،

هڪ ندي ڪل ڪل وهي ٿي،

پر تڪڙو گذري ويندو،

اِهو پل اِلاهي آهي

مُشڪ جا جادوگر سوداگر،

ٻيهر ملنداسين،

تنهنجيءَ سِڪ جي نشي آ ترسايو.

مان سسُئي آهيان، جنهن چنڊ جي

طاقت ڪي قابو ڪيو،

پر ننديپٽ ۾ بامبڙا،

پائيندي سُور ڪي نَ وساريو،

مان تَہ نئون ڄاول ۾ار هُيُس،

جڏهن هُنن صندوق ۾ بند

ڪري نديءَ ۾ ڦٽو ڪيو،

دلُوراءِ ڪان دُور،

ليڪ وڌاتا جو ڪيئن چُڪايان؟

منهنجا ماتا پتا

نائون ۽ ماندر

مونکي پيار ڪندا هئا،

پر مون ڪي پاڻ ڪان

پري موڪليائن،

پنڊت جي اڳڪٿي جا

منهنجي ڪومل اکين مان

ظاهر ٿي

"هيءَ مسلمان سان شادي ڪندي"

هُن ڄيو ۽ منهنجن

مائٽن جو ڌرم ڏکيو

اڙي ائين نَ ٿي!

تَہ مان تارن سان

ڳالهيون ڪرڻ لڳس،

ستارا منهنجا رهنما ٿيا،

۽ مون ڪي تو ڏانهن چڪيندا آيا،

هاڻ مان تو ڪي پنهون پٿر دل

نڪرين ۾ ڳوليهان تي،
پيل رڻ جي ريت ۾ مون ڪي
گهُٽي پر ڪوبہ
برينگ مون ڪي هارائي نہ سگهندو پنهون
منهنجا پيارا،
مُشڪ جا جادوگر سوداگر،
ڀيهر ملنداسين،
تنهنجي سِڪ جي نشي آ ترسايو!

پُنهون

منهنجي پياري،
مون تنهنجي تلاش هر هنڊ ڪئي،
بلوچستان جي اُباٽڪي
جبل چوٽ تان،
جت مون ڪي سپ
ڪيچ مڪران جو راجڪمار،
آري ڄام جو پُٽ ڪري سجاٽين،
پر منهنجو وجود تہ تون آهين،
مان هنا، ماٺري چوٽ سپ،
آر پار لنگهي آيس،
ٿٿي جي راھ ڏانهن،
رتوڙي ۽ ربينون وڪٽندي،
تنهنجيءَ سونهن جي وڪاٽ،
هئي منهنجو رهبر،

ء هي واپاريءَ جو ويس،

بٽيو منهنجي جسم جو حصو،

نہ هئا مون كي كي زيور،

مون كي ڳولها هئي هك سِك رتن جي،

جا هئينءَ تون،

جنهن كي مون پائي وجايو،

مون محمد ڏوڀيءَ جو نالو بڊو هو،

جو ينيور ۾ قبيلي جو سردار هو،

كيئن تون صحيح سلامت،

نديءَ جي تيز وهكري كان بچيئنءَ،

خدا بٽيو تنهنجو نگهابان،

ڏوڀيءَ تنهنجي پتا

جو روپ ڏارڻ كيو،

ڏينهن كجهہ جيان كتبا ويا،

ء چرخو مون طرف وڏندو آيو،

منهنجي دل تنهنجي پريم جي كجن

ڏاڳن ۾ اٽكي.

تنهنجو چند جهڙو چهرو

آ منهنجو رهبر ستارو،

سسُئي منهنجي پياري،

سُرڳ روپي آكاش كولِ

تہ مان تو ۾ سمائجي ويان.

سسُئي

پنهون منهنجا راجکمار،

مان توکي ہڏان ٿي،

اُنهيءَ رڍ جي هير

جيئان جا هلڪي سان ڪن

تي سُٽائي ٿي،

پر منهنجي مٿان

آ هيءُ ڪنور آسمان،

۽ زمين تي پيرن

مان رت زار زار وهي،

مون توکي مُرکندو ڏٺو،

مان جبل جي چوٽ تان

اڳتي وڌيس

۽ تون لاپتا ٿي وئين،

دوُر هڪُ ڪاروان ڏسان ٿي،

ڪاش، مان اُٺ جي اڪ

ھر واريءَ جو ڪٽو هجان،

جيڪو توکي منهنجي قريب آڻي،

تنهنجا ڪاروان ڏسي،

مان خوشيءَ وچان گد گد،

جڏ ڪي جنم گذري ويا

توکي ڏني!

جڏ خوشي هڪ انوکي عطر

جي بوتل ھر بند،

اهڙا اجوبا مون نَہ ڏِنا نَہ پُڊا!
سِپُن جون مالھائون،
بلوچ جا چوڙا،
ڪومل ۽ نازڪ،
سترنگي رنگن ۾ جڙيل،
پر مون ڪي تات تنهنجي،
منهنجي خوشي صرف تون،
تنهنجي سامهون سڀ هيرا
جواهر اصل ڦڪا،
توسان ملڻ ڪو
سُرڳ جو سئر هو،
منهنجي لاءِ تو سوين
تياڳ ڪيا ڪلندي ڪلندي!
مُشڪ جا جادوگر سوداگر،
ٻيهر ملنداسين،
تنهنجيءَ سِڪ جي نشي آ ترسايو!

پنهون
سسئي منهنجي پياري،
ڇا منهنجي سُپنن ۾
تنهنجو آواز آهي؟
ڪنن تي ڪو ڊنڊلو پرلاءِ،
پر تون ڪٿي آهين؟
ڏوڀي گھاٽن ۾

مان ڪيڏو نہ خوش هُيس،
انتظار هوندو هو گهر پهچي
تنهنجو ڪلمُڪ چهرو پسان!
قبيلي جي سردار مون ڪي
ڏوهي ناهي چَڊيو
منهنجي نيهن ڪي پرڪَڻ لاءِ،
۽ ڪپڙا ڏوئڻ جي هُنر تپاسڻ لاءِ
"هيءُ اسانجي ذات جو ناهي"
محمد چيو،
مون ڪي هُن ڪي غلط
ثابت ڪرڻو هئو.
سسُئي تون ڪيڏي تہ سياڻي هئينء،
مون ڪي تہ ڏوئڻ جي جاڻ نہ هئي،
مان تہ ڪپڙا قاڙيندو رهيس،
پر ڪنهن بہ شڪايت نہ ڪئي،
هر قاتل ڪپڙي ۾
هڪ سونو سِڪو لِڪايو،
اسانجي پيار لاءِ سون تہ
نندي قيمت هئي،
ڪي ڪپڙا اُڪڙيا،
تہ ڪا وڏي ڳالھ ناهي،
پر اسانجي پريت جا ڳوپا پُختا ٿيا!
محمد سان مون وادو ڪيو،
تہ مان پنيور ۾ ئي رهندس،

أُتي رھڻ منھنجي لاءِ سولو هئو،
هونءَ بہ پنھنجي راڄ وڃي نہ سگهان هان،
منھنجي دل جي راڻي تہ،
هتي گهائن ۾ هئي.
اسان جا ٿھ ٿھ ڪندا ٿھڪ،
ملايم گجيءَ جيان وڏندا رهيا،
ءِ ڏينهن ڪلندي گذري ويا،
سسُئي اسان خوشيءَ ۾ رڌل ءِ بي فڪر
جيستائين منھنجا پائر آيا،
تو هنن ڪي ڪيڏو نہ پيار ڏنو،
پر هنن اسان سان زيادتي ڪئي،
ڏوهي گهائن تي ڪنهن پراڻي
ڪپڙي جيان نپوڙيو،
اسان جي جيون جي تند نَّي،
چُنرا، هوتو، نوتو...
توهان هيءُ ڇا ڪيو؟
سسُئي مون تي يقين ڪر،
جڏهن اُنهيءَ رات هو
مون ڪي نشي ۾ اُٿ تي چاڙهي
ڪٽي ويا،
مون شراب ڪانہ پيتو هو،
منھنجي پيالي ۾ نشيلي مدرا هئي،
جيڪا هنن ڪي خبر هئي،
تنھنجو چند جهڙو چهرو.

آ منهنجو رهبر ستارو،
سُئي منهنجي پياري،
سُرڳ روپ آڪاش ڪول،
تہ مان تو ۾ سمائجي وڃان.

سُئي

منهنجي دل ٽڪرا ٽڪرا ٿي آهي،
چيڪي مٽيءَ جي چوڙي جيان،
اسان جي پيڙا بي انت آهي،
سرسوتي نديءَ جي خوشبوءِ،
هڏ هڏ ۾ سمايل،
پر ڪاري رات ۾ لومڙ شڪار ڪن،
۽ قدرت پاڻ دشمن ٿئي،
هوا جنهن تنهنجي پيرن جا
نشان ڍاهي ڇڏيا،
۽ سج تہ نہ لهڻ جي ضد تي آ،
پرندڙ آڪاش ٽڏي هوا سُٽڪي،
چنڊ جا ڪارا پاڇا پون،
هنن گرهڻ لڳل ٽڪرين تي
رچ، ڀاندر، ڀگڙ
سڀ منهنجا رستو روڪين،
پر جيسين جان آهي،
لڏيل مسافر جي چولي ۾
مون ڪي اڳتي هلڻو آ، پنهون،

جيسيتائين مان تو كي نَ ڏسان،

منهنجي اُچ نَ مَٽندي.

هڪ پل لاءِ اُميد جاڳي،

ٻِهي جبل جي چوٽ تي،

جتان پاٽي زور سان

وهيو هڪ ٽڪرائتي دڙ مان،

تنهنجو سُهڻو چهرو چلكيو،

مون ڏانهن مُڙكيو،

مون تنهنجو چهرو هڻن ۾ پريو،

تنهنجي روحاني طاقت

تيزيءَ سان منهنجي چهري ۾ اُتي،

چشمو اُچلي موتي

منهنجي پيرن تي اُباٽڪي واريءَ جي وچ

مان ڏيري ڏيري مبوهر پهتس،

جتي هڪ ٽڪريءَ مان نندي جهوپڙي

نظر آئي،

دل ۾ وري اُمنگ جاڳي،

نوكيلي دڳ تي هڪ،

ٻيو ماٺهو ايندو ڏنو،

پر پنهون، هيءُ ريدار،

هن جي نظر تہ خراب آ،

مان تہ هن جي رِڍ ناهيان،

مون هن كان پاٽي گهريو،

۽ جڏهن هو وريو،

مون پيگوان کي ياد کيو، پنهون
مون عرض کيو تہ مون کي ھن کان بچائي،
ءَ ٽڪري ٻن حصن ۾ ٿني،
مان، مان ڌرتيءَ جي گرڀ ۾ سمائجي ويس،
مُشڪ جا جادوگر سوداگر،
ڀيهر ملنداسين،
اسين الله سان گڏجي ھِڪ ٿينداسين.

پنهون

زمين چيرجي پئي آهي
منهنجي پيرن هيٺان،
تنهنجيءَ غيرحاضريءَ
مون کي ماري ڇڏيو،
سسُئي مان تو کي لوچي لهان،
مان موٽي ايندس،
منهنجا پائر
اُميد تہ مون کي وجڊ ڏيندا،
راجا، منهنجي پتا
چاهيو تہ مان هُن وٽ وڃان،
پر هو مون کي مرندو
سهي نہ سگهندو،
تہ مان پڇان ٿو تہ مان توکي
هٿي وٽي اچان،
جيئن کيچ مڪران کي،

تون پنهنجو سمجهي.
ويرانو سڌي رهيو آهي،
مان وجان ٿو،
سيني کان تکڙو اٿ ڳولهي،
منهنجا پائر ٽيئي دغاباز،
چا مون سان ٿيندا... هو
آري چام کي نه ميڇٽ جي
جريئت نه کندا،
منهنجي من جي گرم منظر ۾
سسُئي تون کبڙ وٽ
جيان مضبوط بيني آهين،
پر هو مبوهر ۾ چا آهي؟
او ريديار، هيءَ کهڙي سنت
جي قبر آ؟ تازي ءَ مٽي آلي!
هيءَ ريشمي کپڙي جو ٽکڙ
جيکو زمين تان نظر ٿو اچي؟
کنهنجو آ؟ مون ته پڪ پنيور ۾
ڏٺو آ،
هيءَ ته سسُئي جو رئو آ.
پر هت کيئن پهتو؟
ريديار، مون کي پنهنجي کهاٽي ٻڌائي
مان توکي پنهنجي
داستان ٻڌائيندس،
سسُئي تون هت آهين چا؟

هيُ سناتو مان
سهي نہ سگھندس،
زمين زور سان ڏڏي،
بنا يرڙ لڳا،
مان چير مان پيرن سان اندر كريس،
مٿي سُرڳ كلڻ جا آسار،
هيٺ زمين ۾ ريدار جا پير،
آسمان ۾ چند چمكيو
هلندڙ واريءَ وچ،
ها سسُئي، هاڻ مان توكي
ٻڏان ٿو،
پاڻ كي بہ ٻڏان ٿو،

پنهون تون مون وٽ آيو آهين، هاڻ مان نہ سكندس،
چاكاڻ تہ اسان ٻئي الله سان هك ٿيا آهيون.

The Fire Within

*Go without 'Self', seek no support
and forget everything.*

*Sohini, thy love alone thee to
the other side will bring.*

The Fire Within

Mehar
We are all made of unbaked clay,
hardened in pits of fire.
The wheel, relentless,
spins and turns and burns
and moulds the clay,
while the Great Potter in the sky
watches silently.
I have felt the heat,
been thrown and hollowed out,
filled the vacuum with the scent of love.
Through the dance of the Sculptor's hands,
I stayed pure and true.
How could it be otherwise
since the centrifugal force
was you?

Sohini
We have spun
in different orbits for too long
and you feel alien in these
roaring currents and rocky streams,
dissolving in my arms
as I clutch you tight.
The swollen river has been a familiar foe,
but I have braved it every night
with thoughts of you keeping me afloat.

Tonight, we are far from the kiln
in this in-between watery world.
The *magarmacch*
is waiting with its jaws aslant.
Stay, stay, my love,
do not turn to mud.
The Great Potter is building
a new vessel for us
in eternity.

Mehar
Like the Ravi and Chenab
before they came together,
we have traversed separate paths.
I have turned to mud and then to clay,
been rounded and whole,
broken into shards.
In my journey to you, I have been shaped
in ways I never imagined.

From Bukhara to Punjab
as the river flowed,
I turned my back on the rigid banks
of my father's love;
he begged me not to go.
I was his only offspring,
born with the blessing of a holy man
and though I grew up with wealth,
the stories I heard
of your glittering land
fired up my veins.
I did not know then

that you were my lodestar,
my journeys would lead to your door.
I, Izzat Beg,
have been many things,
and though my name is now mud
I hope I am still worthy of you.

Sohini
Mud and clay for me are the beginning,
the source of all that is good and true,
for Tula Kumbhar's workshop was my playground
and the graceful curves of his pots filled our home.
From him, I learned to fire up the earth,
capture deer and unicorns in vibrant glaze.
Our *martbans* tickled the tongues of nobility;
our *chatis* slaked thirsty throats in all the land.
As I grew, the furnace burned within me;
I learned to forge my own path.
Sohini, they called me, the beautiful one,
and Tula Kumbhar tried to mould me like his pots,
protect me from dazzled men
who tried to buy me like earthenware.

Only you, Izzat Beg, felt true love,
sending your servants to buy so much
that you ran into debt, became
my father's servant instead.

Mehar
So blinded I was by my love for you,
so desperate for the sight of your face
that I could not go back to Bukhara.
I set up my shop close to your home,

sold the merchandise cheap
so that I could come back to buy more,
catch a glimpse of your lovely face.
I have no regrets, Sohini,
for now, I've been through it all.
The four stages of life
are well past me,
and our love has survived till the last.

First, I was the youthful bearer of bangles,
merchant of merchandise for outward show,
trying to win your love.
Then, the hard-working scraper of silt,
scouring the banks to feed Kumbhar's kiln.
It broke my back,
for I was unused to such toil.
Then your father, in his kindness,
spun the wheel once more for me;
made me herder of buffaloes and named me Mehar.
Though living like this
took getting used to,
it was from them I learned contentment,
how to wallow in the mud.
Those mountains were peaceful,
and grass rejoiced on the land.

But when I lost you,
I had nowhere to go.
The forests beckoned,
bedraggled seekers called.
With them, I wandered
through thickets and thorns,
and found my peace,

or so I'd thought, Sohini,
on the bank far away from your home.
Here, under these *sattvic* skies,
the spirits rested;
for a while,
this was where I belonged.

Sohini
I, too, should have been content,
married to Damma, fulfilling
my father's wish – a man so crass
I could never give myself to him.
I thought of you, Mehar,
praying every night that he would not touch me;
strangely, he slipped into slumber and never did.
I have belonged only to you.
Aristocrat, labourer, buffalo herder, fakir at my door–
wherever life takes you, whatever you may be,
you are the one who has lived in my veins,
and Jhulelal has been on our side.

I did not mind, Mehar,
that you, the *jogi* who sacrificed all,
could no longer swim across the river's jaws.
Why did you feed me your own flesh
when there was no fish on a stormy night?
I hungered for you, my love,
but only for your heart,
when I had gladly given mine.

Mehar
My heart is yours, but my body too,
and the wound on my leg will heal.

My only regret, Sohini,
is that you braved the midnight river
instead of me, making the perilous journey
to my side of the bank,
unafraid of those who might see you,
The vessel you trusted
should have kept you afloat;
instead it crumbled in the squall,
and I could do nothing, Sohini,
to keep you safe.

Sohini
The vessel I held last night
was not the one that had always
brought me to you.
It was made of unbaked clay;
no fire touched its being.
Damma's sly sister
had replaced my *surahi*
with one that would dissolve,
and though my *odhni* rode
with the wind, billowing into a sail,
the tempest caught me unawares.
The pot in my arms
dissolved in the roaring waves.
It was the sound of your flute
in the distance that gave me strength and hope
but I was no match
for the rocks that smashed my head.
Mehar, my love, your music
is all that survives.

The storm has subsided now
and you are by my side.
We will cross the bank
just one last time.
The Great Potter waits to greet us.

We are no longer made of unbaked clay
and the furnace has cooled
but within, the fire glows forever.

अंदरि जी आगि

मेहर

असां सभि अणपकल चीकी मिटीअ
मां ठहियल आहियूं,
बाहि जे बठीअ में सख़्तु
थिया आहियूं,
बेरहम चकु घुमे थो, फिरे थो,
घुमे थो, ब्रे थो,
पोइ ग़ोहियल आलीअ मिटीअ
खे आकारु ड़िए थो,
हू शानाइतो कुंभरु ख़ामोशि थी
उभ मां निगरानी करे थो,
मूं उहा तपति महिसूसि कई आहे,
मूंखे खोखिलो करे उछिलियो वियो आहे,
पर मूं उहो ख़ालु तुंहिंजीअ
महक सां भरियो आहे
उन्हीअ नक़ाश जे हथनि जे
नाच पारां
मां पाकु ऐं सचो रहियुसि,
इन खां सवाइ ब्रियो
जिते तूं मर्क़ज़ी ताक़त हुजीं,
उते ब्रियो कुझु कीअं थो थी सघे, सुहिणी?

सुहिणी

असां घणो वक़्तु जुदा गर्दिश जे
घेरे में घुमिया आहियूं, तूं हाणे उन्हननि खां पाण
खे परे महिसूस करे रहियो आहीं,
हाणि तूं हिननि गजकार कंदड़
सीर ऐं पथिराओं वहिकरे में

मुंहिंजे आगोश में समाइजी वञु
ऐं मां तुंहिंजे भाकुर में भरिजी वञा
हीअ फूकियल नदी त
असांजी ज़ातल दुशिमनु आहे,
पर मूं दिलेरीअ सां रोज़ि राति
हीअ पारि कई आहे,
तुंहिंजे ख़्यालनि में लीनु
मां वहिकरे में तरंदी रहियसि,
अजु असां हुन खूड़े खां
दूरि आहियूं,
हिन वहंदड़ वहिकरे में,
मगरमछु लालची वातु फाड़े डिसे थो
इन्तज़ार में!
तरिसु तरिसु…. मुंहिंजा पिरीं,
मिटीअ ड़ांहुं न मुड़ु,
शानाइतो कुंभरु असां लाइ
नओं अमरता जो बासणु
अड़े रहियो आहे.

मेहर

रावी ऐं चिनाब जीआं
बई हिकु थियण खां अगु
असां पिणि अलगि अलगि दग
ते हलिया आहियूं
मां मिटीअ मां
चीकी मिटी बणियो आहियां,
घुमंदो, फिरंदो, छिपुनि
सां टकिराईंदो टुटो आहियां ,
रूप मटाया आहिनि
मूंखे त इन्हीअ जी कल्पना बि
कान हुई,
बुखारा खां पंजाब ताईं,
नदीअ जी रवानीअ सां,
मूं कठोर किनारनि खां
मुंहं मोड़ियो....

मुंहिंजे पीउ प्यार मां पुकारियो,
हुन मिन्थूं कयूं मूं खे
रोकण लाए,
मां त हुन जो सिकीलधो बारु हुयिसु,
घणियुनि संतनि, फ़कीरनि जे
दुआउनि खां पोइ ज़ाओ हुयिसु,
तोड़े मां धन दौलत विच पलियुसि,
तुंहिंजे सोनी धरतीअ जूं कहाणीयूं
बुधी मुंहिंजी रग रग बेचैनि थी,
तड़हिं मूंखे इहा ज़ाण कोन हुई

तूं मुंहिंजी मंज़िलि, किस्मत जो सितारो हुईयं
जो मुंहिंजो सफ़रु तुंहिंजे दर ते पहुंचाईंदो

मूं, इज़्ज़त बेग़,
घणेई वेस मटिया आहिनि, हाणे मुंहिंजो नालो
मिटीअ में मिलियलु आहे
उमेद त मां अ्आ तुंहिंजे लाइकु आहियां....

सुहिणी

मिटी ऐं कची मिटी त आलामत आहिनि,
ऐं वसीलो आहिनि सच ऐं सुठाइअ जा,
मुंहिंजे पीउ तुला कुंभर जो कारिख़ानो
मुंहिंजीअ रांदि जो मैदानु हो,
ऐं संदसि गोल घड़नि सां
असांजो घरु भरियलु हो,
मूं पीउ खां खूड़े में बाहि ब़ारणु सिखी,
मां कल्पना में ख़्याली हरणि पटड़ण लग़सि
असांजियूं ठाहियल खटाणि जूं बरनियूं ऐं कूला
त अमीर रईसज़ादनि खे ललिचाईंदा हुआ,
ऐं बिना हथनि जा रंगीन प्याला
सभिनी जी उऊ लाहींदा हुआ
जीअं जीअं मां वड़ी थियसि
मुंहिंजे अंदर में इहा बाहि ब़री,
मां पंहिंजी राह पाण उणणि लग़सि
मूंखे सभु सुहिणी सुंदरता जी मूर्त सड़ीदां हुआ,
ऐं तुलो कुंभर मूंखे पंहिंजनि घड़नि
वांगुरु क़ालिब में घड़णु चाहियो

पंहिंजे रूप में रचणु चाहियो,
मूंखे मर्दनि जी लालची नज़रुनि खां बचाइणु चाहियो,
जेके मूं खे ठिकर यां चीनीअ जीआं
ख़रीद करण पिया चाहिनि

इज़्ज़त बेग़ सिर्फ़ तूं ई सचे प्यारु जो अहिसासु हुएं
पंहिंजनि नौकरनि हथां मुंहिंजे पीउ
वटां एतिरो सारो सामान ख़रीदु कयइ
जो तूं संदसि कर्ज़दारु थी
नौकर बणिजी पिएं

मेहर

मां तुंहिंजे मोह में एतिरो त अंधो ऐं लाचारु हुयिसु
तुंहिंजो हसीनु चहिरो ड्रिसण खां सवाइ
बुखारा मोटी न सघियुसि,
मूं पंहिंजो दुकानु तुंहिंजे घर जे वेझो खोलियो,
ऐं सभु सामानु सस्ते में विकियो
जीअं त मां ब्रिहर अची मालु ख़रीदु करियां,
ऐं तुंहिंजीअ सूंहं जी हिक झलक पायां, सुहिणी,
मूंखे को बि अफ़सोसि नाहे,
छो जो मूं सभु सठो आहे,
जीवन जा मुख्य चारि दौर
मां पुठियां छड्डे आहियो आहियां,
ऐं असांजी प्रीति आख़िरि ताईं
हरि हालात मां गुज़िरी आहे, बची आहे,
पहिरीं मां चूड़ा, कंगण विकिरंदड़ नौजवान होसि,
ब्रियनि लाए सामानु विकिरण वारो

बाहिरां वापारी पर अंदर में तुंहिंजो प्यारु
पाइण जी आस ऐं प्यास,
पोइ खुरिपो खणी पाणीअ में वहंदड़ि
मिटीअ खे कढण, वारो महिनती,
ऐं साफ़ करण बैदि
कुंभर जे वाड़े में विझणु
मुंहिंजी पुठी सूर में टुटी पवंदी हुई.
मां त अहिड़नि कमनि करण ते हिरियलु न होसि,
पोइ तुंहिंजे पीउ भलाई करे
मूंखे मेंहूं चारण मोकिलियो
नंओ नालो रखियाईं मेहर!
जेतोणिक इहो जीवन जीअण में वेल लग़ी,
मूंखे हुननि ड़ींहनि में खुशी मिली
मिटीअ में लेथिड़ियूं पाइण जी मौज माणी,
जबल पिणि सांतीका हुआ,
ज़मीन ते गाहु बि खुशि हुओ,
पर जड़िहिं मूं तो खे विञायो,
मां किथां जो बि न रहियुसि
का बि जग़ह न सुझी,
झंग इशारा करण लग़ा
टिड़ल पखड़ियल तालिब सड़ण लग़ा
उन्हननि सभिनि सां गडु मां भिटिकियुसि,
वणनि जे झुंडनि ऐं कंडनि में
खुशी मिली
या इहा मुंहिंजी खुशिफ़हिमी हुई, सुहिणी,
नदीअ किनारे तुंहिंजे घर खां दूरि,
हिन पवित्र आकाश हेठां,

मुंहिंजी रूह थोरो आराम कयो,
मां इतां जो आहियां,
हीअ मुंहिंजी मंज़िलि आहे.

सुहिणी

मूंखे पिणि राज़ी थियणु घुरिजे हा,
ड़म सां शादी करे , पंहिंजे पीउ
जी इच्छा पूरी करे.... पर हू
माणिहू त छसो हुओ... मा पाणु
अर्पणु करियां?
मेहर मूं तो बाबति वीचारियो
हरि राति ईश्वर खे ब्राड़ाईंदी हुयसि
त ड़मु मूं खे न छुहे,
ऐं हैरत जी ग़ालिह इहा आहे त हुन
खे रोज़ि निंड अची वेंदी हुई ऐं
मां हुन जे छुहाउ खां बची वेंदी हुयसि

मां सिर्फ़ तुंहिंजी आहियां,
अमीरु वड़ो माणिहू पोरिहियतु,
मेंहूं चारण वारो, फ़क़ीरु हाणे मुंहिंजे दर ते,
ज़िंदगी जिते बि वठी हले, तू कुझु बि हुजीं,
मुंहिंजीअ नस नस में फ़क़्तु तू समायलु आहीं,
जल जो देवता झूलेलाल सांईं असां सां साथु आहे.
मेहर मूंखे को बि ऐतिराजु नाहे,
त तूं जोग़ी बणिजी सभु तियाग़े,
हाणि नदीअ जी तिखी सीर में
तरी न थो सघीं, जे तूं मूं लाए मछी पकिड़े न सघें

त तो पंहिंजो मासु कपे मूंखे
छो डिनो?
मां तुंहिंजे लाए तड़िफंदी रहियसि
महिबूब,
सिर्फ तो लाए बेचैनि,
मूं त पंहिंजी दिलि खुशीअ सां
तोखे डिनी हुई

मेहर
मुंहिंजी दिलि, मुंहिंजो जिसिमु
तुंहिंजो आहे,
टंग जो घाव छा आहे?
भरिजी वेंदो,
सुहिणी मूंखे हिकु अफ़िसोसु आहे
त तूं बहादुरीअ सां अधि राति
ऊंदहि में मूं ड्रांहुं निकितीअं
तोड़े इहो जोखम वारो सफ़रु त
मूंखे करिणो हुओ, मुंहिंजे नदीअ
किनारे ड्रांहुं,
तूं बेबाकु,
जहिं घड़े ते तो विश्वासु कयो
केरु तोखे डिसे उहा
परिवाह न कयइ
उहो त तो खे पारि पहुचाए सघे हा,
पर उहो त भुरी चूरि थी पियो
उन्हीअ ज़ोरदार तूफ़ान में,
ऐं मां लाचारु, सुहिणी तो खे महिफ़ूज़ि
करण लाए कुझि बि करे न सघियुसि.

सुहिणी

कल्ह राति जेको घड़ो मूं झलियो,
उहो सागियो कोन हुओ,
जिहं खे बुधी मां रोज़ि तरी
राति जो तो वटि ईंदी हुअसि

हीउ त कची, अणपकल मिटीअ
जो ठहियलु हुओ,
कहिं बाहि हिन घड़े खे
छुहियो ई कान हुओ,
डुम जी चालाक भेण मुंहिंजो,
घड़ो मटाए छड़ियो
ऐं हीउ कचो घड़ो रखियांई
जे को जल्द भुरी वियो,
जेतोणिक मुंहिंजो रओ हवा में तेज़ीअ सां उड़ामियो
सरह वांगुरु
तूफ़ान जी हलचल मूं खे घेरे छड़ियो
ऐं मां बेवसु थी पियसि
गर्जंदड़ छोलियुनि में घड़ो मुंहिंजीअ
बाहुनि में भुरी वियो,
दूरि खां तुंहिंजीअ मुरलीअ जे
मधुरु आवाज़ मूंखे उमेद ऐं
सघ डिनी,
पर मां छोलियुनि सां
पुज़ी न सघियसि, जेके मुंहिंजे
मथे ते ज़ोर सां लगियूं
मेहर मुंहिंजा प्यारा तुंहिंजो संगीतु

ई आहे हाणे बचियलु,
तूफ़ान बि घटियो आहे,
ऐं तूं मूं साणु आहीं,
असां ब़ुई गड़िजी तरंदासीं

बसि हिकु आख़िरी भेरो
हू शानाइतो कुंभरु असांजी
आजियां करण लाए इन्तज़ार में
बीठो आहे,
खूड़ो पिणि थधो थी वियो आहे
पर असांजे अंदर जी आगि
सदाईं चिमिकंदी रहंदी

اندر جي آگ

ميهر

اسان سڀ اٽڪل چيڪي مٽيءَ

مان تھيل آھيون،

باھ جي بٽيءَ ۾ سخت

تپيا آھيون،

بي رحم چڪُ گھمي تو، قري تو،

پوءِ ڳوھيل آليءَ مٽيءَ

کي آڪار ڏئي تو،

ھوُ شانائتو ڪُنيٖر خاموش ٿي

اِب مان نگراني ڪري تو،

موُن اُھا تپت محسوس ڪئي آھي،

موُن کي ڪوڪلو ڪري اُچليو ويو آھي،

پر موُن اُھو خال تنھنجيءَ

مھڪ سان ڀريو آھي

اُنھيءَ نقاش جي ھٿن جي

ناچ پاران

مان پاڪُ ۽ سچو رهيُس،

اِن ڪان سواءِ ٻيو

۽ جتي تون مرڪزي طاقت هجين،

اُتي ٻيو ڪجھ

ڪيئن تو ٿي سگھي، سهٽي؟

سُهٽي

اسان گھٽو وقت جدا گردش جي

گھيري ۾ گھميا آهيون،

تون هاٽي اُنهن ڪان پاڻ ڪي

پري محسوس ڪري رهيو آهين

هاڻ تون هنن گجڪار ڪندڙ

سير ۽ پٽرائون وهڪري ۾

منهنجي آغوش ۾ سمائجي وڃ،

۽ مان تنهنجي ياڪر ۾ پرجي وڃان

هيءَ ڦوڪيل ندي ته

اسان جي ڄاتل دشمن آهي،

پر مون دليريءَ سان روز رات

جو هيءَ پار ڪئي آهي،

تنهنجي خيالن ۾ لين

مان وهڪري ۾ ترندي رهيس،

اچ اسان هُن ڪوڙي ڪان

دُور آهيون،

هن وهندر وهڪري ۾،

مگر مچ لالچي وات قاڙي ڏسي تو

اِنتظار ۾!

ترس ترس.... منهنجا پرين،

مٿيءَ ڏانهن نَ مُڙ،

شانائتو ڪُنير اسان لاءِ

نئون امرتا جو باسڻ

اڏي رهيو آهي.

ميهر

راوي ءِ چناب جيئان

بئي هڪ ٽيڀ ڪان اڳ،

اسان پٽ الڳ الڳ دڳ

تي هليا آهيون،

مان مٽيءَ مان

چيڪي مٽي بڻيو آهيان،

گهمندو، ڦرندو چپن سان ٽڪرائيندو

ٽڪرن ۾ ٽٽو آهيان،

روپ مٽايا آهن

مون ڪي تہ اِنهيءَ جي ڪلپنا بہ

ڪانہ هئي،

بخارا کان پنجاب تائين،

نديءَ جي روانيءَ سان،

مون ڪنور ڪنارن کان

منهن موڙيو،

جڏهن منهنجي پيءُ پيار مان پُڪاريو،

هن منٿون ڪيون مون ڪي

روڪڻ لاءِ،

مان تہ هن جو سڪيلتو ڀار هُيس،

گهٽين سنتن فقير جي

دعائن کان پوءِ جائو هُيس،

توڙي مان ڏن دؤلت وچ پليس،

تنهنجي سونيءَ ڏرتيءَ جون کهاٽيون

ٻَڌي منهنجي رڳ رڳ بيچئن ٿي،

تڏهن مون کي اِها جاڻ ڪونه هئي

ته تون منهنجي منزل --قسمت جو ستارو هئيئن،

جو منهنجو سفر تنهنجي در تي پهچائيندو،

مون، عزت بيغ

گهٽيئي ويس مٿيا آهن،

هاٽي منهنجو نالو مٿيءَ ۾ مليل آهي،

اُميد ته مان ايا تنهنجي لائق آهيان.

سُهڻي

مٿي ۽ کچي مٿي ته علامت آهن،

۽ وسيلو آهن سچ ۽ سنائيءَ جا،

منهنجي پيءُ ٽلا ڪُنير جو ڪارخانو

منهنجيءَ راند جو مئدان هو ،

ء سندس گول گهڙن سان

اسان جو گهر پريل هو،

مون پيءُ کان کوڙي تي باھ ٻارڻ سکي

مان کلپنا ۾ خيالي هرڻ پٺيان لڳس،

اسانجيون ناهيل کٽاڻ جون برنيون ۽ ڪُولا

تہ امير رئيسزادن کي للچائيندا هئا،

ء بنا هٿن جا رنگين پيالا

سيني جي اُڃ لاهيندا هئا،

جيئن جيئن مان وڏي ٿيس،

منهنجي اندر ۾ اِها باھ ٻري،

مان پنهنجي راھ پاڻ اُڻڻ لڳس.

مون کي سڀ سُهڻي سُندرتا جي مورت سڏيندا هئا،

ء ٽلو ڪُنير مونکي پنهنجن گهڙن

وانگر قالب ۾ گهڙڻ چاهيو،

پنهنجي روپ ۾ رچڻ چاهيو،

مونکي مردن جي لالچي نظرن کان بچائڻ چاهيو،

جيڪي مون کي نِڪر يا چينيءَ جيئان

خريد ڪرڻ پيا چاهن،

عزت بيغ صرف تون ئي سچي پيار جو احساس هُئين،

پنهنجن نؤكرن هٿان منهنجي پيءُ

وٽان ايترو سارو سامان خريد كيئ،

جو تون سندس قرضدارٿي پئين،

نؤكر بٽجي پئين.

ميهر

مان تنهنجي موه هر ايترو تہ انڌو ۽ لاچار هُيس،

تنهنجو حسين چهرو ڏسڻ كان سواءِ

بخارا موتي نہ سگهيُس،

مون پنهنجو دكان تنهنجي گهر جي ويجهو كوليو،

۽ سپ سامان سستي هر وكيو،

جيئن تہ مان ٻيهر اچي مال خريد كريان،

۽ تنهنجي سونهن جي هك جهلك پايان، سُهٿي،

مون كي كوبہ افسوس ناهي،

چو جو مون سپ سنو آهي،

جيون جا مكيہ چار دؤر

مان پنيان چڏي آيو آهيان،

۽ اسان جي پريت آخر تائين

هر حالت مان گذري آهي، بچي آهي،

پهرين مان چوڙا، ڪنگڻ وڪڻندڙ نوجوان هوس،

هينِ لاءِ سامان وڪڻ وارو

ٻاهران واپاري پر اندر ۾ تنهنجو پيار

پائڻ جي آس ۽ پياس،

پوءِ ڪرپو ڪٽي پاٽيءَ ۾ وهندڙ

مٽيءَ ڪي ڪيڏ وارو محنتي

۽ صاف ڪرڻ بعد

ڪنير جي واڙي ۾ وجهڻ،

منهنجي پُني سوُر ۾ ٿئي پوندي هئي،

مان تہ اهڙن ڪمن ڪرڻ تي هريل نہ هوس،

پوءِ تنهنجي پيءُ يلائي ڪري

مون ڪي مينهون چارڻ موڪليو،

نئون نالو رکيائين ميهر،

جيتوٽيڪ اِهو جيون جيئڻ ۾ ويل لڳي،

مون ڪي هنن ڏينهن ۾ خوشي ملي،

متيءَ ۾ ليٽريون پائڻ جي مؤج ماڻي،

جبل ۾ سانتيڪا ٿئا،

زمين تي گاھ ۽ خوش ٿئو،

پر جڏهن مون توکي وجايو،

مان ڪتان جو ۽ نہ رهيس،

ڪا ۽ جڳھ نہ سُجھي،

جهنگ اِشارا ڪرڻ لڳا،

نڙيل پڪڙيل طالب سڏڻ لڳا،

اُنهن سيني سان گڏ مان پنڪيس،

وٽن جي جهنڊن ۽ ڪنڊن ۾
خوشي ملي،

يا اِها منهنجي خوشفهمي ٿئي، سُهڻي،

نديءَ ڪناري تنهنجي گھر ڪان دُور،

هن پوتر آڪاش هينان،

منهنجي رُوح ٿورو آرام ڪيو،

مان اِتان جو آهيان،

هيءَ منهنجي منزل آهي.

سُهڻي

مون کي پڻ راضي ٿيڻ گھرجي ھا،

ڈمر سان شادي کري، پنهنجي پيءُ

جي اِڇا پوري کري..... پر ھوُ

ماڻھو تہ چسو ھئو..... مان پاڻ

ارپڻ کريان؟

ميهر مون تو بابت ويچاريو،

ھر رات ايشور کي ھاڈائيندي ھيس،

تہ ڈمر مون کي نہ ڇھي،

۽ حيرت جي ڳالھہ اِھا آھي تہ ھُن

کي روز نندِ اچي ويندي ھئي ۽

مان ھُن جي ڇھاءُ کان بچي ويندي ھيس.

مان صرف تنهنجي آھيان،

امير وڈو ماڻھو ھاٿي پورھيت،

مينھونچارڻ وارو، فقير ــ منهنجي در تي،

زندگي جتي بہ وٿي ھلي، تون کُجھُ بہ ھجين،

منهنجيءُ نس نس ۾ فقط تون سمايل آھين،

جل جو ديوتا جهوليلال سائين اسان سان ساڻ آهي.

ميهر مون کي کو ٻ اعتراض ناهي،

تہ تون جوڳي ٻڌجي سپ تياڳي،

هاڻ نديءَ جي تڪي تير ۾

تري نٿو سگهين، جي تون مون لاءِ مڇي پڪڙي نہ سگهين

تہ تو پنهنجو ماس ڪپي مون کي

ڇو ڏنو؟

مان تنهنجي لاءِ تڙڦندي رهيس،

محبوب، صرف تو لاءِ بيچئن،

مون تہ پنهنجي دل خوشيءَ سان

توکي ڏني هئي.

ميهر

منهنجي دل، منهنجو جسم

تنهنجو آهي،

ٺنگ جو گهاءُ ڇا آهي؟

ڀرجي ويندو،

سُهڻي مون کي هڪ افسوس آهي

تہ تون بهادريءَ سان اڄ رات

اونڌ ۾ مون ڏانھن نڪتينءَ،

توڙي اِھو جوکم وارو سفر تہ

مون ڪي ڪرڻو ھئو، منھنجي نديءَ

ڪناري ڏانھن،

تون بي باڪ،

ڪير توکي ڏسي أھاپرواھ نہ ڪيءَ،

جنھن گھڙي تي تو وشواس ڪيو،

أھو توکي پار پھچائي سگھي ھا،

پر أھو تہ پُري چوُر ٿي پيو

أنھيءَ زوردار طوفان ۾،

ءِ مان لاچار، سُھڻي توکي محفوظ

ڪرڻ لاءِ ڪُجھہُ بہ ڪري نہ سگھيس.

سُھڻي

ڪلھہ رات جيڪو گھڙو مون جھليو،

أھو ساڀيو ڪونہ ھئو،

جنھن ڪي ھڻي مان روز تري

رات جو تو وٽ ايندي ھئس،

هيءُ تہ ڪچي، اڏ پڪل منيءَ

جو نهيل هئو،

ڪنهن باھ هن گهڙي ڪي

جُهيو ئي ڪانہ هئو،

ڏم جي چالاڪ ييڙ منهنجو

گهڙو مٺائي چڏيو،

۽ هيءُ ڪچو گهڙو رڪيائين

جيڪو جلد پُري ويو،

جيتوٽيڪ منهنجو رئو هوا مر تيزيءَ

سان اڏاميو سرھ وانگر،

طوفان جي هلچل مون ڪي گهيري چڏيو

۽ مان بيوس ٿي پيس،

گرجندڙ چولين مر گهڙو منهنجيءَ

ٻانهن مر پُري ويو،

دوُر ڪان تنهنجيءَ مرليءَ جي

مڌر آواز مون ڪي اُميد ۽

سگهہ ڏني،

پر مان چولين سان

پڇي نَ سگهيس، جيڪي منهنجي

مٽي تي زور سان لڳيون،

ميهر منهنجا پيارا تنهنجو سنگيت

ئي آهي هاڻي بچيل،

طوفان بہ گهتيو آهي،

۽ تون مون ساڻ آهين،

اسان ۾ئي گڏجي ترنداسين،

بس هڪ آخري ٻيرو

هوُ شانائتو ڪُنِير اسانجي

آجيان ڪرڻ لاءِ اِنتظار ۾

ٻينو آهي،

ڪوڙو پِٽ ٺَڏو ٿي ويو

پر اسان جي اندر جي آگ

سدائين چمڪندي رهندي.

Princess of Illusion

Where need one drive the camel
when great radiance reigns all around?
In my being is Kak – in me
gardens and springs abound...

Princess of Illusion

Moomal
They knew me as the Princess of Illusion
behind labyrinthine walls and a lake of glass,
a maze where many suitors were lost.
They were fools, Rano – all fools,
and deserved what they got,
hunting me down like a deer,
riding to Lodhruva,
believing they were worthy of me.
Kak was my refuge,
my magic and mystery,
a mirage for all but the best.
The veils of the world were many,
but it was here that I found true love.
No one else was good enough, Rano,
and though you believe I've deceived you,
you are still my king, I, your queen.
Let us make the right moves, beloved.
This game of chess is one that both can win.

Rano
Yes, they were fools, my Moomal,
but so were you.
I, too, rode to Kak, through river banks
that were littered with graves
of princes, saints, nobles, ascetics,
who never returned from your land.
The gardens were enchanting,
but enchanted too,

with twisted trees that wove their arms
around unsuspecting throats.
These men braved it all for you,
beating the drum you placed outside your walls.
as though victory was theirs already.
Who knew that your servant, Natur,
would entwine them in your maze?

And there were those who fainted
at the fake tigers that roared,
others who plunged into roiling waters
above the flimsy bridges you built,
rested their tired backs
on cots that collapsed
into wells below.
Yes, they were foolish,
but so was I,
believing you would be
faithful to me.

Moomal

What could we have done?
My father, King Nand of Mirpur Mathelo –
he lost his fortune because of my silly mistake.
I believed the yogi who asked for help,
saying he was ill and the only cure
would be the magic swine's tooth
that my father had entrusted to me.
Where this swine had walked,
the waters receded.
My father killed the beast,
parted the waters
and buried his treasure
where no one else would see.

But this yogi turned out to be a thief
and took it all.
My father would have killed me
but Soomal came up with a plan
and we built Kak to recover his wealth.

Rano
I threw a betelnut
at the glistening waters of Kak
and when it bounced back
I knew it was just glittering glass.
Did you think its watery sheen
would fool me?
How then, did I end up
being fooled by you?

We had travelled far –
Hameer Soomro, my king,
and the other ministers of Umerkot,
Seenharro and Daunro,
my friends, though not my equals
as I learned at Kak.
Our hunts took us to distant lands,
and adventure was all we sought,
a little excitement when the deer in the forest,
were not challenge enough for us.
So when, in the woods, we met
a prince in ragged clothes,
who spoke of how you robbed him,
how he wandered confused in the maze
in your palace of illusion,
and managed to escape with his life,
we knew that Kak would be our next conquest,

or at least it would be mine.
The journey was long, Moomal,
but Kak, with its gems and stratagems,
dazzled in the Thar,
duplicitous, like you, and yet,
mine alone,
or so I had believed.

Moomal

We saw you, my sisters and I,
and I knew you were the one,
so handsome, so determined
to make it through.
Your companions were not good enough,
not even your king;
they fell to Soomal's wiles.
But you, whose weapon was a betelnut,
knew well that things
are never what they seem.
We have known the joy
of streaming rivers,
felt flowers come alight
on these fertile banks
but every sunrise, dear Rano,
I wilted when you had to leave.

Rano

It was my jealous king who stopped me,
yet every night, I wore my magic spurs
and flew to you. The desert dunes
were no match for my wings of flame.
Your luminous face was the lamp
that led the way. We had but

a few short hours before I returned
but they were enough
to light my sky at dawn.
The king found out,
and imprisoned me.
He would have had me killed,
but his queen, my sister,
urged him to set me free.
and so I returned, Moomal,
risking my life for you
and found you were not alone.
Who was it, my love?
Who lay beside you,
in garb that resembled mine?
I would have beaten him,
and you, with my walking stick,
but I merely left it behind
so you would know that I was there.

Moomal
What could I have done, Rano?
Like a riverbed abandoned
I thirsted for you every night,
waiting for the thunder
of camel hooves,
but silence crumbled
upon my palace walls instead.
Where once the euphoric
shorelines swelled,
the soil had turned to sand.
That was Soomal, my sister,
Rano, who lay by my side
lending me warmth

until you came back.
You should have trusted me,
my love; instead,
like the Indus changing course,
you left.

It has been months now
since I came searching for you,
disguised as a man,
making Umerkot my home
until I saw your face again.
Did you not realise, Rano,
that it was me?

Let us play chess
just one last time
and set the game on fire.
If it is endgame for us,
I choose the Kiss of Death!

Rano
Moomal, always the Princess of Illusion,
where have you disappeared?
What have you done?
Life may have separated us;
in Death, we will unite.

But tell me, love,
in this game of chess,
did either one of us win?

मायावी राजकुमारी

मूमल

हू मूंखे मायावी राजकुमारी करे चवंदा हुआ,
भितियुनि मां मुंझाईदड़ रस्ता ,
मायावी शीशे जूं ढंढूं
मुंझाईदड़ मांडाणा
केतिरा सदिरिया लापता थी विया,
राणा, हू सभु मूर्ख हुआ... असुलु मूर्ख,
सो ई पलइ पियुनि
मुंहिंजो हथु वठण पिया चाहीनि,
जणु त मां हरणु हुअसि
लड़ाणे डुंहुं घोड़ा खणी
अंधी आस में
काकु मुंहिंजो अझो हुओ
मुंहिंजे जादूअ जो राजु,
सभिनि लाए रुझ
पर सभि खां बहितरीन
दुनिया जा रूप अनेक,
पर हिते ई मूं पंहिंजो सचो रूप ड्ठिो
राणल, बियो केरु तो जहिड़ो सुठो न हुओ,
तोड़े तूं सोची थो
मूं तो सां दोखो कयो,
तूं मुंहिंजो राजा आहीं,
मां तुंहिंजी राणी,
प्रीतम, अचु त वरी कदम अग्रिते वधायूं,
हीअ शतरंज जी बाज़ी बुई खटी सघूं था.

राणो

हा, मुंहिंजी मूमल हू सभु मूर्ख हुआ,
पर तूं बि नादानु निकितींअ,
मा पिणि काक तरफ़ सुवारु थियुसि,
नदियूं ओणाघे जिते कएं दफ़न हुआ
राजकुमार, संतनि, पीर, जोग़ी ,
जे तुंहिंजे वतन मां सालिम कीन मोटिया,

बाग़ मोहित कंदड़ जादूई हुआ,
बेशक़ सभु तिलिस्मी हुआ
वकिड़ियल वणनि संदनि ब्राहूं क़ाबू कयूं

अणज़ातलनि संदनि सिर
हिननि माणहुनि सभु कष्ट सूर्हियाई सां सठा,
फ़क्त तुंहिंजे लाए मूमल
जेके नग़ारा तो दीवारूनि ते लग़ाया हुआ,
हुननि ज़ोर ज़ोर सां वज़ाया,
ज़ुणु त का सोभ हासिलु कई हुअनि,
कंहि खे ख़बर हुई त तुंहिंजी दासी नातर,
हुननि खे तुंहिंजे माया ज़ार में मुंझाईंदी ?
ब्रिया के त नकुली शींहं जी
गजगोड़ बुधी बेहोश थी विया,
किनि मेरी गप में भरियल पाणीअ
में टिपो ड्रिनो बिना समझ जे
तुंहिंजीअ अड़ियल पुलि मथां,
तुंहिंजीअ कचे सुट सां मड़िहियल खट ते वेठा
वञी सिधो ऊन्हे खूअ में पिया,

हा मूमल हू सभु ड्राढा विसूरा हुआ,
पर मां बि त अणज़ाणु होसि
ऐतिबारु कयमु त तूं
मूं सां वफ़ा कंदीअं.

मूमल
असां छा करे सघूं हा?
मुंहिंजो पीउ मीरपुर मथेले जो राजा नंदु,
हुन पंहिंजी सज़ी पूंजी विआई,
मुंहिंजीअ चुक जे करे,
मूं त मदद घुरण वारे जोग़ीअ
ते विश्वास कयो,
जोग़ीअ ब़ाड़ायो हू बीमारु आ,
फ़क्त सूअर जे जादूई ड़ंद सां ठीक थींदो,
उहो ड़ंदु मुंहिंजे पीउ मूंखे संभालण
लाए ड़िनो हुओ,
जिते जिते सूअर वियो पे,
पाणी सुकंदो वियो,

मुंहिंजे पीउ सूअर खे मारियो,
पाणीअ खे धार कयाई,
समूरो ख़ज़ानो दरियाह जे पेट में दफ़न कयाई,
जितां केरु बि खणी न सघे,
हीउ जोग़ी त चोरु निकितो,
सज़ो मालु मिलिकियत चोरी करे वियो,
मुंहिंजो पीउ त मूंखे मारे छड़े हां,
मूंखे देस नेकाली मिली

सूमल हिक रिथ रची,
असां हिते अची काक महलु अड़ियो,
ख़ज़ानो वरी हासिलु करण लाए.

राणो

मूं काक जे चिमकेदारु पाणीअ
में सोपारी उछिली,
उहा टकिराइजी मोटी आई,
मां समुझी वियुसि इहो
शफ़ाफ़ु कांचु आहे,
तो खे छा लग्रो इन्हीअ शीशे जो जादू
मूं खे मूर्ख बणांईंदो ?
ख़बर नाहे पोइ मां तुंहिंजे हथां
कींअ बेवकू फ़ थी पियुसि?
असां वड़ो सफ़र तइ कयो...
हमीर सूमरो, मुंहिंजो राजा,
ऐं बियो उमरकोट जा अमलदार
सींअहरो ऐं डुउंणो,
मुंहिंजा दोस्त, जेतोणिक मुंहिंजे
बराबरीअ जा कीन हुआ,
शिकार लाए असां दूरि पहुतांसी,
मन में इच्छा हुई क हिं जांबाज़
विंदुर जी,
हिक अजीब बेताबी,

जड़िहिं जंगल में हरणु डिठो सीं,
संदसि शिकारु असां लाए मामूली हो
अग्रिते झंग में लीरुनि में

हिकु राजकुमारु ग़ड़ियो,
जंहिं बुधायो त कीअं तो हुन खे लुटियो,
कीअं हू मुंझाईदड़ राह में भिटिकियो,
तुंहिंजे मायावी महल में,
जीअं तीअं करे पंहिंजी जानि बचायांईं,
असां उन्हीअ पलु सोचे छड़ियो
असांजी अग़ीं मंज़िल काक थींदी,
घट में घटि मूं पक कई
काक ते पहुचण जी,
मूमल सफ़रु ड़ाढो डिघो हुओ,
पर काक महलु हीरनि ऐं जवाहरनि
सां पे चिमिकियो
तो जीअं चालिबाज़!
तो खे हासिलु करण जी
सिर्फ़ मुंहिंजी ख़ुशिफ़हिमी निकिती

मूमल
असां तो खे ड़िठो,
मूं यकदमि ज़ातो, त उहो तूं ई आहीं,
एड़ो ठाहूको जुवानु,
अटलु इरादेवारो
जेको पक ई सोभ पाए सघे,
तुंहिंजा साथी त हीणा नज़र पे आया,
न ही तुंहिंजो राजा बहादुरु हुओ,
पर राणल तूं बहादूरु राजा निकितें,
हू सभु त सूमल जे फंदे में फाथा,
तुंहिजो हथियारु सिर्फ़ु सोपारी हुई,

तो खे सज़ी ख़बर हुई,
त जेको ड्रिसण अचे
सो सचु नाहे,

असां प्रेमियुनि खे वहंदड़ि नदियुनि
जी खुशीअ जो अहिसासु आहे,
असां गुलनि खे टिड़ंदो ड्रिठो आहे,
हिननि आबाद किनारनि ते,
पर हरि रोजु सिजु उभिरण वक़्तु
प्यारा राणा तो खां मोकिलाइण वक़्तु
मां कोमाइजी वेंदी हुअसि.

राणो
मुंहिजे सारीले राजा मूं खे रोकियो,
पर मां हरि राति जो पंहिंजी जादूई
घोड़े ते तो वटि उड़ामी ईंदो होसि,
बयाबान जे वारीअ जो ढेरु मुंहिंजीअ
अंदिरूनी आगि ऐं उड़ाम सां
पुज़ी न सघिया,
मूमल प्यारी, तुंहिंजो नूरानी चेहिरो ,
मुंहिंजी जोति बणी राह ड्रेखारींदो रहियो,
असां वटि कुझु कलाक हुआ
मोटी वञण लाए,
पर उहे काफ़ी हुआ

आखिर राजा खे ज़ाण पइजी ई वेई
मूंखे कैद कयाई,

हू त मूं खे माराए छड्डे हां,
पर हुन जी राणी, मुंहिंजीअ भेण,
हुन ते ज़ोरबार आंदो
हू मूंखे आज़ादु करे,
मां मोटी आयुसि, तो वटि, मूमल!
पंहिंजीअ जानि जी बाज़ी लगाए
अची छा डि़सां त तूं अकेली कान्ह हुईयं,
तुंहिंजे पासे में ब्रियो को सुम्हियल हो
उहो बि मुंहिंजे लिबास में,
मां त हुन खे मारे छड्डियां हा,
तो खे बि,
मां लकुणु उते छड्डे आयुसि,
जीअं तो खे पतो पवे त मां आयो होसि

मूमल

राणा! मां छा करे सघां हा?
कहिं वेगा़णीअ नदीअ जे
किनारे जीआं,
मां हरि राति तो लाए तड़िफ़ंदी रहियसि,
उठ जे खुड़ियुनि जे आवाज़
बुधण लाए तरसियल,
पर ख़ामोशी ई भुरी पेई
मुंहिंजे महल जे भिति ते,
जिति कड़हिं किनारो खुशीअ सां बहकंदो हो,
हाणे उते सब्ज़ मिटी जुणु
वारी बणिजी पेई,
राणल! हूअ त मुंहिंजी,

भेण सूमल मूं सां सुम्हयल हुई,
तुहिंजे अचण तांई,
मूंखे आथतु ड्रियण लाए
तो खे मूं ते एतिबारु करणु घुरिजे हा,
पर प्यारा! तूं सिंधूअ नदीअ वांगुरु
वहिकरो बदिलाए हलियो विएं,
केतिरा महिना लंघे विया,
तोखे ग़ोल्हींदे, ग़ोल्हींदे,
मां वेसु मटे मर्द जी पोशाख में,
उमरकोट में पंहिंजो घरु बणायो,
जड्ढिं तुहिंजी मोहींदड़ि शिकिल नज़र आई,
राणल छा तो मूंखे सुञातो ई न!
उहा मां हुयसि, अचु त वरी
शतरंज जी रांदि खेड़ियूं,
हिकु आख़िरी भेरो,
चालि जो जोशु बक़रारु रहे
असांजे लाए पछाड़ीअ जी बाज़ी आहे,
मां मौत जी चुमी चूंडियां थी

राणो

मूमल हमेश मायावी राजकुमारी,
तूं किथे ओझल थी वेईअ?
ज़िंदगीअ असांखे ज़रूर जुदा कयो,
मौत में असां हिकु थींदा सीं,
हीउ शतरंज जो खेलु
केरु खटे थो?

ماياوي راجكماري

مومل

هُو مون كي ماياوي راجكماري كري چوندا هئا،
پتين مان منجهائيندڙ رستا،
ماياوي شيشي جون ڏنيون
منجهائيندڙ مانڊاٽا
كيترا سدريا لاپتا ٿي ويا،
راٽا هُو سڀ مورک هئا .... اصُل مورک،
سو ئي پلئَ پيُن جنهن جي لائق هئا،
منهنجو هٿ ونڌ پيا چاهِن،
جِٽُ تہ مان هرڻُ هئس،
لڏاٽي ڏانهن گهوڙا كٽي،
انڌي آس ۾،

كاكُ منهنجو اُجهو هئو،
منهنجو جادوءَ جو رازُ،
سيني لاءِ رُج،
پر سڀ كان بهترين،
دنيا جا روپ انيک،
پر هتي ئي مون پنهنجو سچو روپ ڏنو.
راٽل ٻيو كير تو جهڙو نہ هئو،
توڙي تون سوچين ٿو
مون تو سان دوكو كيو،

تون منهنجو راجا آهين،
مان تنهنجي راڻي،
پريتم اڄُ ت وري قدم اڳتي وڌايون،
هيءَ شطرنج جي بازي هِئي ڪِئي سگهون ٿا.

راڻو
ها منهنجي مومل هوُ سپ ت مورک هئا،
پر تون ب نادان نڪتينءَ،
مان پڻ ڪاڪ طرف سوار ٿيُس،
نديون اورانگهيجتي ڪئين دفن هئا،
راجڪمار، سنت، پير، جوڳي،
جي تنهنجي وطن مان سالم ڪين موٽيا،

باغ موهت ڪندڙ جادوئي هئا،
بيشڪ سپ طلسمي هئا،
وڪڙيل وٽن سندن ٻانهون قابو ڪيون،
اڌ جاتل سندن سِر،
هنن ماٿن سپ ڪشٽ سورهيائي سان سٺا،
فقط تنهنجي لاءِ، مومل
جيڪي نغارا تو ديوارن تي لڳايا هئا،
هنن زور زور سان وڃايا،
جڻ ت ڪا سوپ حاصل ڪئي هئن،
ڪنهن ڪي خبر هئي ت تنهنجي داسي ناتر،
هنن ڪي تنهنجي مايا ڄار ۾ منجهائيندي؟

بيا ڪي تہ نقلي شينهن جي
ڳجگوڙ ٻڌي بي هوش ٿي ويا،
ڪن ميري، ڳپ ۾ پريل پاٽيءُ
۾ ٿيو ڏنو بنا سمجھ جي،
تنھنجيءُ ڪچي سُت سان مڙهيل ڪٽ ٿي وينا
تہ وڃي سِڌو اونھي ڪوھ ۾ پيا،
ها مومل هُو سپ تہ ڏاڍا وسورا هئا،
پر مان بہ تہ اٽڪاڻ هيس،
اعتبار ڪيم تہ تون
مون سان وفا ڪندينءَ.

مومل
اسان چا ڪري سگھون ها؟
منھنجو پيءُ ميرپور مٿيلو جو راجا نند،
هن پنھنجي سڄي پونجي وڃائي،
منھنجيءُ چُڪ جي ڪري،
مون تہ مدد گھرڻ واري جوڳيءُ
تي وشواس ڪيو،
جوڳيءُ ٻاڌايو هُو بيمار آ،
فقط سوئر جي جادوئي ڏند سان نيڪ ٿيندو،
اُهو ڏند منھنجي پيءُ مون ڪي سنيالٽ
لاءِ ڏنو هئو،
جتي جتي سوئر ويو پئي
پاٽيسُڪندو ويو،

منهنجي پيءُ سوئر کي ماريو،
پاٽيءَ کي ڏار کيائين،
سمورو خزانو درياھ جيپيٽ ۾ دفن کيائين،
جتان کير بہ کٽي نہ سگهي،
هيءُ جوڳي تہ چور نڪتو،
سڄو مال ملڪيت چوري ڪري ويو،
منهنجو پيءُ تہ مون کي ماري ڇڏي ها،
پوءِ مون کي ديس نيڪالي ملي،
سومل هڪ رت رچي،
اسان هتي اچي ڪاڪ محل اڏيو،
وري خزانو حاصل ڪرڻ لاءِ.

راڻو
مون ڪاڪ جي چمڪيدار پاٽيءَ
۾ سوپاري اُڇلي،
اُها ٽڪرائجي موٽي آئي،
مان سمجهي ويس اهو
شفاف ڪانچ آهي،
توکي چا لڳو اِنهيءَ شيشي جو جادو
مونکي مورک بڻائيندو؟
پوءِ خبر ناهي مان تنهنجي هٿان
ڪيئن بيوقوف ٿي پيس؟
اسان وڏو سفر طئہ ڪيو....
حمير سومرو، منهنجو راجا،

۽ پيو عمرڪوٽ جا عملدار،
سينهرو ۽ ڏوئنرو،
منهنجا دوست، جيتوٽيڪ منهنجي
برابريءَ جا ڪين هئا،
شڪار لاءِ اسان دُور پهتاسين،
من ۾ ِاچا هئي ڪنهن جانباز
وندر جي،
هڪ عجيب بيتابي،

جڏهن جهنگل ۾ هرڻ ڏنوسين،
سندس شڪار اسان لاءِ معامولي هئو
اِڳتي جڏهن جهنگ ۾ ليرُن ۾
هڪ راجڪمار گڏيو،
جنهن ٻڌايو تہ ڪيئن تو هن ڪي لٿيو،
ڪيئن هُو منجهائيندڙ راھ ۾ ٻنڪيو،
تنهنجي ماياوي محل ۾،
جيئن تيئن ڪري پنهنجي جان بچايائين،
اسان اُنهيءَ پل سوچي ڇڏيو تہ
اسان جي اِڳين منزل ڪاڪ تي ٽيندي،
گهٽ ۾ گهٽ مون پڪ ڪئي
ڪاڪ تي پهچڻ جي،
مومل سفر ڏاڍو ڏکو هئو،
پر ڪاڪ محل هيرن ۽ جواهرن سان پئي چمڪيو
تو جيئان چالباز!

توکي حاصل ڪرڻ جي
صرف منهنجي خوشفهمي نڪتي.

مومل

اسان توکي ڏنو،
مون يڪدم ڄاتو، تہ اُهو تون ئي آهين،
ايڏو ٿاهوُڪو جوان،
اتل اِرادي وارو،
جيڪو پڪ ئي سوڀ پائي سگهي،
تنهنجا ساٿي تہ هيٺا نظر پي آيا،
نہ هي تنهنجو راجا بهادر هئو،
پر راڌل تون بهادر راجا نڪتين،
هوُ سڀ تہ سوُمل جي قند مِ قاتا،
تنهنجو هٿيار صرف سوپاري هئي،
توکي سڀ خبر هئي،
تہ جيڪو ڏسڻ اچي
سو سچ ناهي،

اسان پريمين ڪي وهندڙ ندين
جي خوشيءَ جو احساس آهي،
اسان گلن ڪي نئڙندو ڏنو آهي،
هنن آباد ڪنارن تي،
پر هر روز سڀ اُيرڻ وقت
پيارا راٺا

توکان موکلائڻ وقت
مان کومائجي ويندي هيس.

راڻو

منهنجي ساڙيلي راجا مون کي روکيو،
پر مان هر رات جو پنهنجي جادوئي
گهوڙيتي تو وٽ اُڏامي ايندو هوس
بيابان جي واريءَ جو ڍير منهنجيءَ
اندروني آگ ۽ اُڏام سان
پُڄي نہ سگهيا،
موملپياري، تنهنجو نوراني چهرو
منهنجي جوت بڻي راھ ڏيکاريندو رهيو.
اسان وٽ کجھ کلاک هئا
موٽي وڃڻ لاءِ،
پر اُهي کافي هئا.

آخر راجا کي ڄاڻ پئجي ئي ويئي
مون کي قيد کيائين،
هُو تہ مون کي مارائي چڏي هان،
پر هُن جي راڻي، منهنجيءَ پيڳ،
اُنتي زوربارآندو
هُو مون کي آزاد کري،
مان موٽي آيس تو وٽ، مومل
پنهنجيءَ جان جي بازي لڳائي
تنهنجي خاطر،

اچي چا ڏسان ته تون اڪيلي ڪانه هئينءَ،
تنهنجي پاسي ۾ هيو ڪو سُهيل هئو؟
أهو به منهنجي لباس ۾،
مان ته هُن ڪي ماري چِڙيان ها،
توکي به،
مان لڪٽ أتي چڙي آيس،
جيئن توکي پتو پوي ته مان آيو هوس.

مومل

راٽا مان چا ڪري سگهان ها؟
ڪنهن ويڳاٽيءَ نديءَ جي
ڪناري جيئان،
مان هر رات تو لاءِ تڙقندي رهيس،
أٽ جي ڪڙين جي آواز
هڌ لاءِ ترسيل،
پر خاموشي پُري پيئي
منهنجي محل جي يٽ تي،
جت ڪڌهن ڪنارو خوشيءَ سان ٻهڪندو هو،
هاڻي ڪڌهن أتي سبز مٽي جٽ
واري ٻٽجي پيئي،
راٽل هوءَ ته منهنجي
پيٽ سُومل مون سان گڏ سُهيل هئي،
تنهنجي اچڻ تائين،
مونکي آٽت ڏيٽ لاءِ،

توکي مون تي اعتبار کرڻ گهرجي ها،
پر پيارا تون سندوءَ نديءَ وانگر
وهکرو بدلائي هليو وئين،
کيترا مهنا لنگهي ويا،
توکي ڳولهيندي ڳولهيندي،
مان ويس مٽي مرد جي پوشاڪ ۾
عمرکوٽ ۾ پنهنجو گهر بڻايو،
جڏهن تنهنجي موهيندڙ شڪل نظر آئي،
راڻل چا تو مون کي سڃاتو ئي نَ!
اُها مان هيس، اچ ت وري
شطرنج جي راند کيڏيون،
هڪ آخري ڀيرو،
چال جو جوش برقرار رهي،
اسان جي لاءِ ڀچاڙيءَ جي بازي آهي،
مان موت جي ڇمي چونڊيان ٿي،

راڻو
مومل، هميشه ماياوي راجڪماري،
تون ڪٿي اوجهل ٿي ويئينءَ؟
زندگيءَ اسان کي ضرور جدا ڪيو،
موت ۾ اسان هڪ ٿينداسين،
هيءُ شطرنج جو کيل
ڪير کٽي ٿو؟

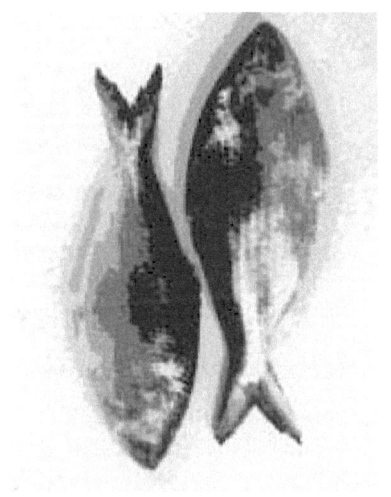

The Keenjhar's Song

Fie upon maids of princely caste

who walk stiff-necked, so haughtily.

Praise to the daughter of the lake,

her true love to the king gave she...

The Keenjhar's Song

Noori
At the Keenjhar, where flamingos were my friends,
and sweet fish resided in the calm waters I called home,
we cast our nets wide and brought back
riches from the River God.
My straw shanty was the palace I always knew,
and gems sparkled at my feet where
the sun touched the shore.
Our boats were fragile against the vastness of the lake,
and the fragrance of fish bones was no match
                              for your rich perfumes,
but Jaam Tamachi, I knew love here, and this was
                              my true wealth.
I know I am blessed to be your *rani* in these
                              rich surroundings,
yet your marble *mahal* is cold to the touch,
and the six Samma queens who came before me
poison the air with their tongues.
Even the birds are silenced here, the warblers I knew,
who brought back tales of the Indus to my fisherfolk.
You cast your net and took me back with you
to Helaya Hill where I did not belong
and I want to return to where I can hear
the Keenjhar's silent song.

Jaam Tamachi
In all of Thatta, that I have ruled for so long,
you are the most precious to me.
It was my good fortune to find you like the lotus
where the moon shone upon the lake

and lit my sail. I have had many queens before you,
wretched creatures with fluttering eyes and painted smiles,
insipid women whose jewels outshine their cheeks,
who will never know the sparkle of your skin.
The Keenjhar has been your treasury;
its waters gleam upon your chiselled face.
By day, the sun ignites your hair,
by night, your eyes become burning sapphires.
Not one of these women holds a match to you.
You are my wealth, the only one who counts.

Noori
And yet you doubted me.
You say I matter, but who knows,
when I grow old, and wrinkles crack my face.
will there be another you will find more dear?
You treat your queens as no more than worthless
playthings in your hands; each vies for your attention
in any way they can. They flutter
their winged eyelashes to catch your distant gaze.
Their tongues are sharp, for they are truly crazed,
lonely amidst the cawing of your flock.
They need you, but all you can do is mock,
and someday, I could be one among them too,
when you find someone younger, fresh and new.

As for my visitor, that has concerned you so.
Yes, my brother has been stealing past the palace gates,
with nothing but the moon to light his way.
He comes when you sleep to help me feel at home,
creeping in and out with a rough wicker basket in his hand.
Your queens insisted that I gave him jewels
                              behind your back,

They have been jealous, with good reason, but you?
You say you love me, yet where is the trust?
You did not believe me when I said this was untrue.
So here, my king, who claims to love me so,
here is the container I have kept for my brother
                                        to take back.
It has nothing but fish bones and grainy crumbs,
the food from home I relish every night.
In your palace, the kitchens overflow,
but the rich mangos and dates will never seem enough,
because on the mud floor of our shanty by the Keenjhar,
I have eaten delicacies you will never know.
The saffron-scented pulaos from your *rasoi*
are no match for the sweet *pallo*
from my mother's wrinkled hand.

Jaam Tamachi
Noori, you are my seventh queen, but will always
                                        be the first;
I have known the others and seen through their
                                        worthless wiles.
On that day of truth, when I said I would take one,
and only one of my queens on an evening out,
they donned rich robes and sought me through
                                        kohl-lined eyes,
but their rouged cheeks and hennaed hands
were rough against my palm.
Not just their faces, but their pockmarked hearts,
fill me with disgust. Noori, the aroma of fish
that seeps through the garments you continue to wear
is richer to me than all the *ittar* in our land.
Only you, whose beauty outshines them all,
need no artifice to seek attention.

Someday, the saints will remember you;
you take pride in yourself, and that is always good,
but your humility and grace
are stronger and truer than anything I have ever seen.
You will outlive us all, Noori,
staying true to yourself, yet humble to the last.

Noori
You must be kinder to the queens;
show them they have been important to you.
How can you value me if the others don't matter, too?
And when you are ready, Jaam Tamachi,
I will join you where the waters flow;
the River God will greet us there.
Let me show you the riches of the forest by the lake,
where we can live eternally without a care.

And to this day, the Keenjhar murmurs
between one heart and another
and the River God is listening
as the sun sets on the water.
The raucous crows of spite and greed
with kohl-lined eyes and pointed beaks
still circle the rocks that line the lake.
They hope their cawing will somehow shake
the quiet depths of the lovers' sleep
but the moon shines on the melody
of songbirds on the rustling reeds
and the waves are gentle on the rocky shore
where the fisherwoman and king lie evermore
and the forest feels alive.

कींझर जो संगीतु

नूरी
कींझर ढंढ ते जिति पाणी पखी
मुंहिंजा साथी हुआ,
मिठियूं मछियूं सांति पाणीअ में
रहंदियूं हुयूं,
उते मुंहिंजो घर हुओ,
असां पंहिंजियूं ज़ारियूं पखेड़े
उछिलाईंदा हुआसीं,
ऐं वरुण देवता जी कृपा सां
मछियुनि रूपी धनु खणी मोटंदा हुआसीं,
कखनि ऐं सुकल गाह जी झूपिड़ी
ई मुंहिंजो महलु हुई,
सिज जा तिरविरा जड़िहिं किनारे ते पवंदा हुआ
मुंहिंजे पेरनि ते हीरनि वांगुरु चिमकंदा हुआ
असांजियूं बेड़ियूं ढंढ जे कुशादगीअ
अगियां नाज़ुकु हुयूं
मछियुनि जी ख़ुश्बूअ जी भेट
तुंहिंजे क़ीमती अतुर सां नथी थी सघे

ज़ाम तमाची मूंखे प्यारु हिते हासिलु थियो
इहा ई मुंहिंजी असुली दौलत हुई
मां ज़ाणियां थी त मां तुंहिंजी राणी बणजी
केड्री त सभाग़ी आहियां,
हिन शाहाणे माहोल में त बि
तुंहिंजो संगमरमरु जो महल त थधो हुओ

छह समियूं राणियूं जे के मूंखां
अग़ि आयूं
पंहिंजीअ तिखीअ ब़ोलीअ सां हवा
में ज़हिरु थियूं फहिलाइनि

हिते त पखी पिणि शांत आहिनि,
जेके लातियूं लिवंदा हुआ
तिनि खे मां ज़ाणा,
जेके सिंधू नदीअ जा नियापा
मुंहिंजनि मुहाणनि लाए आणीदा हुआ

तो पंहिंजो ज़ारु उछिलियो ऐं मूं
खे पाण सां हेलिया टकिरीअ
में वठी आएं,
जहिं सां मुंहिंजो को बि नातो न हो
ऐं मां मोटी कींझर जो ख़ामोश
रागु बुधणि थी चाहियां.

ज़ाम तमाची

मूं सज़े थटे ते चडा साल
राजु कयो आहे,
नूरी तूं मूं लाए ड़ाढी अमुल्ह आहीं,
मां ख़ुशिनसीब आहिया जो तो खे
कंवल जे गुल जीआं हथि कयुमि,
जड़हिं चंड जी चिमकाट थी
ढंढ मथां झिलमिलाई रोशनी फैली
ऐं मुंहिंजी ब़ेड़ीअ जे सरह खे रोशन कयो

तो खां अगु मूं खे
घणेई राणियूं हुयूं,
निंदोरियूं राणियूं ,
हुनिन जूं अखियूं फड़फड़ाईंदियूं हुयूं
ऐं रंडियल नकुली मुश्कूं
बेलुत्कु फिकियूं औरतूं जिनि जा
ग़ुह संदनि जे ग़िलनि जे
भेट में वधीक चिमकिया पिए,
हुनिन खे तुंहिंजे सूरत जे
तेज जी सुधि न हूंदी,
कींझर ढंढु तुंहिंजो ख़ज़ानो आहे,
ढंढ जो पाणी तुंहिंजे तराशियल
चिहरे ते टिमकंदो आहे,
ड़ींहं जो सिजु तुंहिंजे वारनि
सां मचु मचाईंदो आहे,
ऐं राति ताईं तुंहिंजियूं अखियूं
ब़रदंड़ नीलम जहिड़ियूं थींदियूं
हिननि समियुनि राणियूं मा का हिक बि
लाइकु नाहे
तूं मुंहिंजी मिलिकियत आहीं,
तूं मुंहिंजो ख़ज़ानो आहीं
सिर्फ़ तूं ई अहम मुंहिंजे दिलि में आहीं

नूरी
ऐं तंहिं हूंदे बि तो मूं ते
शकु कयो,
हा, रोज़ि राति जो मूं सां मिलण

हिकु शख़्सु ईंदो हुओ,
महल जे दर खां लिकी छिपी
दाख़िल थींदो हुओ,
सिर्फ़ चंड जी रोशनी हिन
सां गड्ड हूंदी हुई,
जड़हिं तूं सुम्हंदो हुएं
हीउ मूंखे आथत डींदो हुओ
हू सुरंदे खिसिकंदे अंदरि ब्राहिरि
ईंदो वेंदो हो,
हिक तीलियुनि जी सादी टोकरी
हथ में खणी

हुननि तो खे बुधायो त
हीउ मुंहिंजो भाउ आहे,
उहे सही हुआ, पर तो खे
मूं ते विश्वासु कीन हो
जेको दब्रो मूं हिन खे ड्रिनो
असांजे नंढे ग्रोठ में खणी वञण लाए,
उन्हीअ में मछीअ जा कंडा
ऐं ढोढे जी भोरि हुई,
न ई हीरा जवाहर चोरी करे,
हितां हिननि वड्डियुनि ख़मोश दीवारुनि मां
खणी पिए भग्रो,
हुननि औरतुनि तो सां कूड़ु ग़ाल्हियो
ऐं तो एतिबारु कयो?
तुंहिजे महल जो रंधिणो तुहिन
सां भरपूरू आहे, का कमी नाहे

पर इहे महंगा अंब ऐं खजूर
काफ़ी नाहिनि,
छो त कींझर जे कप ते मूं
पंहिंजीअ झूपिड़ीअ में जे के लज़ीज
उमदा ताम खाधा आहिनि से
तूं न ज़ाणी
तुंहिंजे रंधिणे में रधियल केसर
जी सुगंधि वारो पुलाउ,
मुंहिंजीअ अमड़ जे गुंजियल हथनि
सां रधियल पले साम्हूं फिको आहे,
उहो पुलाउ कुझु बि नाहे.

ज़ाम तमाची
नूरी तूं मुंहिंजी सतीं राणी आहीं,
पर मुंहिंजे लाए सदाईं ख़ासि आहीं,
मूं हुननि सभिनी राणियुनि खे सुआतो आहे,
मामूली औरतूं, फ़रेबु कंदियूं आहिनि,
तहिं ड़ींहु सचु ज़ाणण लाए
जड़िहिं मूं ऐलानु कयो त मां हिक ई
राणीअ खे शाम जो सैरु कराईंदुसि,
हू सभु महंगा, चिलिकिणा वग़ा पाए आयूं
ऐं कजलु लग़लु अखियुनि
सां मुंहिंजी आस कयनि,
पर संदनि रंग सां थपियल ग़िल ऐं
मेहंदी रता हथ,
मूंखे बनावटी महिसूसि थिया
ऐं मुंहिंजीअ तिरीअ खां पिणि सख़्त लग़ा

न फ़क्त हुनि जा चेहिरा
पर संदनि दाग़दार दिलियुनि मां
मूंखे बुछां आई,
नूरी, मछीअ जो हुग़ाउ जेको
तुंहिंजनि सादनि कपिड़नि मां
टिमंदो आहे उहो हिन सज़ीअ
ज़मीन जे अतुर खां लाजवाबु आहे,
तुंहिंजी सूंहं हुनि खां वधीक
बक़ादारु आहे
तो खे कहिं बि तरतीब जी
गुंजाइशि नाहे,
मुंहिंजो ध्यानु छिकण लाए

कहिं ड्रींहुं, साधू संत पिणि
तो खे यादि कंदा,
तुंहिंजी निमाणाई ऐं ब़ाझ
सदाई लाए पेई ग़ाएबी

नूरी
तो खे पंहिंजियुनि राणियुनि सां
रहमदिलि थियणु घुरिजे;
हुनि खे अहिसासु ड्रियारु त हू
सभु बि तुंहिंजे लाए ज़रूरी हुयूं,
जे तूं हुनि जो लिहाजु न कंदें
त मुंहिंजो क़दरु कीअं कंदें?
ऐं जड़हिं तूं हिन ग़ाल्ह लाए तियारु थींदें ज़ाम तमाची
तड़हिं मां तो सां गुड़िजी हलंदसि
उते जिते कल कल कंदड़ पाणीअ जी धारा में

वरुणु देवता असांजी आजीयां कंदा,
अचु त तो खे ढंढ जे चौधारी
झंग, बेले जो खज़ानो डेखारियांई,
जिति असां हमेशह दाइम क़ाइम रहंदासी.

अजु ड़ींहं ताईं कींझर ढंढु सुसिपुसि
करे ब्रिनि दिलियुनि विचि,
ऐं वरुण देवता असांजी कहाणी बुधे थो,
जीअं जीअं सिजु पाणीअ में लहे थो.
ऐं वड़वाता कांव
लालच ऐं हवस सां भरियलु पूरे सींगार सां सजायल
ढंढ जे मंथा चकर
काटींदा नज़रि अचनि था
शायद इन्हीअ उमेद सां त संदनि कां कां सां
मुहिबनि जी गहिरी, निंड फिटंदी,
चंडु आसमानु रोशन करे
छोलियूं होरियां होरियां
पाथराएं किनारे सां टकिराईनि
जिति मुहाणी ऐं राजा सदाईं
मौजूदि आहिनि
झंगु पिणि ज़िंदह महिसूसि थे थो....
असां खां पोइ बि.........

کينجهر جو سنگيت

نوري

کينجهر ڏنڊ تي جِتِ پاڻي پڪي
منهنجا ساٿي هئا،
۽ مٺيون مڇيون سانت پاڻيءَ ۾
رهنديون هيون،
اُتي منهنجو گهر هئو،
اسان پنهنجيون جاريون پڪيڙي
اُڇلائيندا هئاسين،
۽ وروڙ ديوتا جي ڪرپا سان
مڇين روپي ڏن ڪٺي موٽندا هئاسين،
ڪڪن ۽ سُڪل گاه جي جهوپڙي
ئي منهنجو محل هئي،
سج جا ترورا جڏهن ڪناري پوندا هئا
منهنجن پيرن تي
هيرن وانگر چمڪندا هئا،
اسانجيون ٻيڙيون ڏنڊ جي ڪشادگيءَ
اڳيان نازڪ هيون،
۽ مڇين جي خوشبوءَ جي ٻيٽ
تنهنجي قيمتي عطر سان نٿي تي سگهي،

جام تماچي مون کي پيار هتي حاصل ٿيو
۽ اِها ئي منهنجي اَصلي دؤلت هئي،

مان چاٽيان ٿي تہ مان تنهنجي راتي بٽجي
کيڏي تہ سياڳي آهيان،
هن شاهاٽي ماحول ۾ تہ بہ
تنهنجو سنگمرمر جو محل تہ ٽڏو هئو،

چھہ سميون راٽيون جيڪي مونکان
اڳ آيون،
پنهنجي تکيءَ ٻوليءَ سان هوا
۾ زهر پيون ڦهلائن،

هتي تہ پڪي پٽ شانت آهن،
جيڪي لاتيون لوندا هئا
تن کي مان چاٽان،
جيڪي سنڊوُ نديءَ جا نياپا
منهنجن مهاٽن لاءِ آٽيندا هئا،

تو پنهنجو چار اُڃليو ۽ مون
کي پاڻ سان هيليا ٺڪريءَ
۾ وٿي آئين،
جنهن سان منهنجو ڪوبہ ناتو نہ هو
۽ مان موٽي ڪينجهر جو خاموش
راڳ ٻڌڻ ٿي چاهيان.

چَام تماچي

مون سجي ٿئي تي چڳا سال
راج ڪيو آهي،
نوري تون مون لاءِ ڏاڍي املھ آهين،
مان خوشنصيب آهيان جو توکي
ڪنول جي گل جيئان ھٿ ڪيم،
جڏھن چندِ جي چمڪات تي
ڏنڌ مٿان روشني ڦھلي،
ءِ منھنجي ٻيڙيءَ جي سرھ ڪي روشن ڪيو،

توکان اڳ مونکي
گھٽيئي راڄيون ھيون،
ندوريون ناريون، ھنن جون اکيون ڦِڙڦِڙائينديون ھيون
ءِ رڳيل نقلي مُشڪون،
بي لطف ڦڪيون عورتون جن جا
ڳلھ سندن جي ڳلن جي
پيٽ ۾ وڏيڪ چمڪيا پئي،
ھنن ڪي تنھنجي صورت جي
تيج جي سُڌ نہ ھوندي،
ڪينجھر ڏنڌ تنھنجو خزانو آهي،
ڏنڌ جو پاڻي تنھنجي تراشيل
ڇري تي ٽمڪندو آهي،
ڏينھنجو سج تنھنجي وارن
سان مچ مچائيندو آهي،

ءِ رات تائين تنهنجيون اڪيون،
ٻرندڙ نيلم جھڙيون ٿينديون،
هنن سمين راتين مان
ڪا هڪ بہ لائق ناهي،
تون منهنجو خزانو آهين،
صرف تون ئي اهر
منهنجي دل ۾ آهين

نوري

ءِ تنهن هوندي بہ تو مون تي
شڪ ڪيو،
ها روز رات جو مون سان ملڻ
هڪ شخص ايندو هئو،
محل جي در ڪان لڪي ڇپي
داخل ٿيندو هئو،
صرف چنڊ جي روشني هن
سان گڏ هوندي هئي،
جڏهن تون سمهندو هئين تہ
هيءُ مونکي آڌت ڏيندو هئو،
هُو سُرندي ڪسڪندي اندر ٻاهر
ايندو ويندو هو،
هڪ تيلين جي سادي ٽوڪري
هٿ ۾ کڻي،
هنن توکي ٻڌايو تہ هيءُ منهنجو يارُ آهي،
اُهي صحيح هئا، پر توکي

مون تي وشواس كين هئو،
جيڪو دپو مون هن كي ڏنو
اسانجي نندي ڳوٺ ۾ ڪٽي وچٽ لاءِ،
اُنهيءَ ۾ ميڄءَ جا ڪندا،
ءِ ڌوڌي جي پور هئي،
نَ ئي هيرا جواهر چوري ڪري
هتان هنن وڌين خاموش ديوارون مان
ڪٽي پئي پيڳو،
هنن عورتن تو سان ڪوڙ ڳالهايو
ءِ تو اعتبار ڪيو،
تنهنجي محل جو رنڌٽو طعامن
سان پرپور آهي، ڪا ڪمي ناهي،
پر اِهي مهنگا انب ءِ ڪجور
ڪافي ناهن،
چو تَ ڪينجهر جي ويجهو مون
پنهنجي جهوپڙيءَ ۾ جيڪي لزيز،
عمدا طعام ڪاڏا آهن سي
تون نَ چاٽين،
تنهنجي رسوئيءَ ۾ رڌيل ڪيسر
جي سُڳنڌ وارو پُلاءِ،
منهنجي امڙ جي گهنجيل هٿن
سان رڌيل پلي سامهون ڦڪو آهي،
أهو پُلاءِ ڪُجهہُ ناهي.

چامُ تماچي

نوري تون منهنجي ستين راڻي آهين

پر منهنجي لاءِ سدائين پهرين خاص آهين،

تُنءَ عورتون، فريب ڪنديون آهن،

تنهن ڍينهن سچ جو پاسو ڪندي،

جڏهن مون اعلان ڪيو تہ مان هڪ ئي

راڻيءَ ڪي شام جو سئر ڪرائيندس،

هُو سڀ مهنگا، چلڪٽا وڳا

پائي آيون ءِ ڪاجل لڳل اکين

سان منهنجي طلب ڪين،

پر سندن رنگ سان ثقيل ڳل ءِ

ميهندي رتا هٿ،

مون ڪي بناوٽي محسوس ٿيا

ءِ منهنجيءَ تريءَ ڪان پِٽ سخت لڳا،

نہ فقط هنن جا چهرا پر

سندن داغدار دلين مان

مون ڪي بُجان آئي،

نوري، مِچيءَ جو هِڳاءُ جيڪو

تنهنجن سادن ڪپڙن مان

نِمندو آهي اُهو هن سجيءَ

زمين جي عطر کان لاجواب آهي،

تنهنجي سونهن هنن کان وڌيڪ

جمار ماڻي،

توکي ڪنهن بہ ترتيب جي

گنجائش ناهي منهنجو ڏيان
چڪڻ لاءِ.
ڪنهن ڏينهن، ساڏو سنت پٽ
توکي ياد ڪندا،
تنهنجي نماڻائي ءِ ٻاجھ
اسان سيني ڪي پٽيان چڏيندي.

نوري
توکي پنهنجين راڻين سان
رحم دل تيڻ گهرجي،
هنن ڪي احساس ڏيار تہ هوُ
سپ بہ تنهنجي لاءِ ضروري هيون.
جي تون هنن جو لحاظ نہ ڪندين
تہ منهنجو قدر ڪيئن ڪندين؟
ءِ جڏهن تون تيار آهين جام تماچي،
تڏهن مان توسان گڏجي هلندس
اُتي جتي ڪل ڪل ڪنڊڙ پاٽيءَ جي ڏارا م
وروڻ ديوتا اسان جي آويڳت ڪندا.
اڄ تہ توکي ٻنڊ جي چوڏاري
جهنگ، ٻيلي جو ڏن ڏيڪاريانءِ،
جت اسان هميشھ دائم قائم رهنداسين.

*اڄ تائين ڪينجهر ٻنڊ سُس پُس
ڪري ٻن دلين وچ،*

۽ وروڻ ديوتا اسان جي ڪهاڻي ٻڌي ٿو،
جيئن جيئن سچ پاڻيءَ ۾ لهي ٿو.
۽ وڏ واتا ڪانو
لالچ ۽ حوس سان ڀريل پوري سينگار سان سجايل
ڊنلڙ جي مٿان چڪر
ڪاٽيندا نظر اچن ٿا
شايد اِنهيءَ اُميد ۾ ته سندن ڪان ڪان سان
محبن جي گهڙي، سانت ننڊ ڦٽندي،
چنڊ آسمان روشن ڪري
چوليون هوريان هوريان
ٽتراٽينڪاري سان ٽڪرائين
جت مهاڻي ۽ راجا سدائين
مؤجود آهن
جهنگ پڻ زنده محسوس ٿي ٿو....
اسان ڪان پوءِ به....

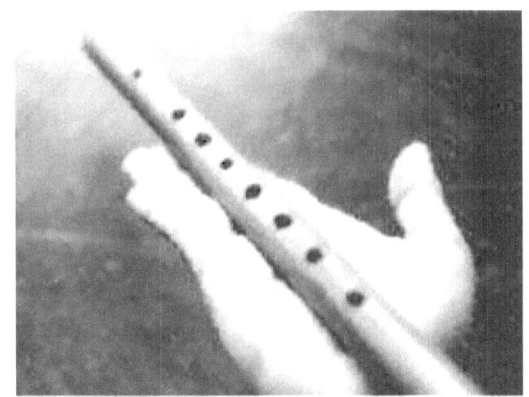

The Flute and the Tree

I'll burn these houses – mansions tall
that shorn of loved ones are.
'All things return to their origin';
that's my longing's call.

The Flute and the Tree

Marui
It has been many years since I have seen my desert land,
Magical Maleer, that heaven in the sand.
You robbed me, Umar Soomro, of the people I love,
The Marus of Panhwar, for whom I was a turtle dove.
You swooped down like a Spotted Eagle,
made me your prey,
imprisoned me in your fort, tried to make me obey.
But you must accept, great king,
I will never belong to you,
because my heart is in the Thar; my parents too.
It was Palino and Maduee who brought me to life,
and I will go back to be Khetsen's wife.

Umar
You precious, obstinate woman, whom I have
                                    wished to make mine.
No one remembers you in the land you hold dear.
No one will ever want you back in Maleer.
If you return, they will only sneer.
Because they will believe you have been defiled
they will no longer see you as their child.
So, take your head out of the sand and listen to me.
I have been in love with you and could have
                                    made you happy
but you continued to see me as your enemy
despite all the wealth I command.
I asked for your hand, to share it with you.
I treated you well and deserved such treatment too.

Marui

To you, my Maleer may be a mirage in the Thar,
But to me, it is real even though I am now so far.
It is a place I have loved, where I have felt whole,
and though years have passed, it is alive in my soul.
My loved ones may have forgotten me,
but in my heart, they will always be
dearer than any riches in your chilly fort
where brick walls close in as you hold court.
You are king and would have me only for sport,
but make no mistake, I will never be your consort!

Umar

You try to make yourself ugly, refuse to wash your hair,
wear your ragged garments, though I have offered
                                        you silk and gold.
You thought by these actions, you could turn me away.
You do not know the power that you could hold
over this youthful body that had waited for you
and while I could certainly have had you by force
there would be no pleasure until you could agree
to take my love and this life of luxury.
Other women would gladly accept these gifts.
What made you so stubborn when you could be free?

Marui

What freedom do you speak of, you cruel monarch,
for I am cocooned in this space where the day seems dark
because though the sun shines, I do not see it
                                        light up my home
and while you have given me fragrant gardens
                                        where I can roam
none of it matters because it is not where I belong,

and however you try to break me, I will stay strong.
Maleer burns like a hot rod in my brain
and I will not rest till I see it again.
One day, you will have to let me go back
to where my people await me, and the world
is not so black,
because in my part of the Thar, emeralds glitter in the field
and no matter what you say, I will not yield.
For me, life in your cold fort holds no charm.
Phogsen, that traitor, who tended our farm,
could not have me, so he did me harm.
With what evil intentions he came to you
and whispered in your ear what you should do.
Were you so gullible, you listened to him
and rode on your camel to Maleer on a whim
so that you could, in the guise of a traveller, appear
and snatch me from the home I held so dear?
Your camel's hooves caused a sandstorm as we flew by
and though my eyes burned, I could not cry.
I beg you, king, that should I die,
take my body back to Maleer so I can say goodbye.
In the end, one must always come home.

Umar
You are no prisoner, but a welcome guest.
I have tried for many years but failed to make you my own,
and this has broken my soul, it is true.
Over these years, my fondness for you has grown.
You are the woman I will always want.
No one else has such a rare power to enchant.
You leave a mark on all you see,
with not just your beauty but your purity.
And though you spurned my love,

you have transformed me.
I must tell you a secret, though I resisted at first.
I have tried to ignore it, but my heart did burst.

Marui
What is it, Umar? You seem perturbed.

Umar
Some days ago, a woman came to me.
She said she knew your family
and she knew mine when I was an infant in arms.
She told me a story I found hard to believe
because to think it true would cause me to grieve.
I shut it from my mind for as long as I could
but in my heart, I knew I was doing no good.
Still, I attempted to make you mine
I knew it was wrong, but could not let you go.
Your resolve has saved us both, and I now know
it is time to take you home myself.

The truth is, Marui, that your mother had fed me.
She was my wet nurse when my parents
                                travelled to Maleer
and I was hungry, but my mother's breast was dry.
Maduee came to my rescue and suckled me as her own.
Marui, you are like my sister, and I must atone
for the sin I have committed, the wrong I have wrought,
believing you to be someone I could have bought.
And I still love you, but it has to be
a different kind of love touched by purity.
I have sent my man to your parents with
                                a message from me,
though I do not know if they will accept my apology.

Marui

Umar Soomroo, is this true what you say?
Then let us go back at once this very day!
I must see my loved ones and the man I will wed,
for it is only Khetsen who will share my bed
and I cannot wait another moment to see them!

Umar

Let us go then, my camel awaits
though I am full of sorrow as you leave these gates.
Come, sister, let us return,
and though my heart will forever yearn
for you, I can sin no more.

Marui

You do well, my king, to let me go.
The truth must have been hard for you to say, I know,
but you have finally earned my love,
and proved to me there is a god above.
Let us make haste, for the desert calls my name.
To delay any further would be a shame
and the sun is already going down.

Umar

I worry that after all these years,
you *baradari* will think you are no longer pure,
and if that happens, dear sister, you will have
                                        a home with me
of that, you can always be sure.
but I will send my army to punish them for doubting you.

Marui
First, you committed a sin by abducting me.
Would you compound that with further brutality?
Go, king, go back, for I see Maleer in the distance;
and this land alone is my reason for existence.
If they doubt me, I will touch a hot iron rod
to prove that I am blessed by the hand of God
and they will know I am chaste of body and soul.

Umar
Then let us go, dear Marui, may the saints be with you
in a world where there are so few
who can love a land that may forget them.
But if they put you to the test,
know that I will be blessed
if I can prove myself too.

And when the sands of suspicion
blew thick and fast in Maleer,
Marui and Umar held out their hands
and the flaming iron rod was cold to their touch.
They emerged unscathed, for both were pure,
The fire was something they could easily endure.

Now, the kinsfolk listened when Marui spoke
the truth she had always known to these simple folk.
"We all belong to the place of our birth
and must return to that heaven on earth
if we have lost our way.
The flute must be one with the wind and the tree
to the space where it found its melody.
Only then is it truly home."

वण हेठां मुरलीअ जो अलापु

मारुई

केतिरा वर्हिय गुज़िरिया
पंहिंजो रिणु पटु ड्डिठे,
जादूई मलीरु ज़णु, वारीअ ते सुर्गु,
उमर सूमरा तो मूंखां मुंहिंजा
माइट छिनिया
जेके मूं खे ड्डाढो प्यारु कंदा हुआ,
पंवहार क़बीले जा मिठिड़ा मारू,
मुंहिंजी हिफ़ाज़त कुमीअ जीआं कंदा हुआ,
तो मूं ते ज़ालिम बाज़
जीआं झटु हयों
पंहिंजो शिकारु बणायो,
पंहिंजे क़िले में क़ैद कयो
मूं ते हुकुमु हलाइण चाहियो
पर राजा, इहा ग़ालिह
त तइ आहे,
मां तुंहिंजी हरगिज़ि न थींदसि
छो जो मुंहिंजी दिल थर में
समायल आहे,
मुंहिंजनि माउ पीउ वटि आहे,
पालणे ऐं माड़ोईअ मूंखे
जनम ड्डिनो,
ऐं मां वापस वरी खेतसेन जी
कुंवारु बणजण लाए आती आहियां

उमर

तूं अनमोल ऐं हठीली नार आहीं
जहिंखे मां पाइणु थो चाहियां,
जिहं मुल्क में तुंहिंजी दिलि लग्री आहे
उते तोखे सभिनि विसारियो आहे
जे तूं मोटी वेंदीअं त हू
तो ते ठठोली कंदा,
तो खे महिणा ड्रींदा,
हू समुझंदा
तू अपवित्र थी चुकी आहीं,
तो खे नंढो ब्रारु करे न लेखींदा
तहिं करे ततलु वारीअ जी ताति छड़ि
ऐं मुंहिंजो चयो मञु,
मां तो सां बेहद मुहबत कयां थो,
तूं ई मूंखे खुशि करे सघीं थी
पर तुंहिजे लाए त मां को
दुश्मनु आहियां,
एतिरी धन दौलत हुजण जे बावजूद
मूं तुंहिंजो हथु झलणु चाहियो
जीअं हीअ मिलिकियत तो सां वंडियां
मां तो सां सुठो वरताउ कयां थो,
उमेद त मां तुंहिंजे चडे
मोट जे लाइकु आहियां

मारुई

तुंहिंजे लाए मलीरु थर जी रुअ हूंदो
पर मुंहिंजे लाए सारो जहानु आहे,
मां भलि कोहें परे आहियां

पर इहो ग़ोठु मूंखे प्यारो आहे,
जिति मूं पाण खे मुकमलु भांइयो आहे,
हालांकि वर्हिय लंघे विया
पर मुंहिंजी रूह अजु पिणि ज़िंदह आहे.
मुंहिंजनि मारूअनि शायद मूंखे विसारियो हूंदो
पर मुंहिंजीअ दिलि में हू सदा रहंदा,
तुंहिंजे सर्दु क़िले जे दीवारुनि
खां वधीक अज़ीज रहंदा
जिते तूं दरिब़ारु लग़ाईंदो आहीं
तू भलि राजा आहीं पर मां
तुंहिंजी रांदि लाए रांदीको नाहियां,
इन्हीअ ग़लतफ़हमीअ में न रहिजंइ
त मां तोसां कड़िहिं विहांउ कंदिस

उमर

तू पाण खे बदशिकिल बणाइण
जी कोशिश करीं थी,
नकी वार धोईं थी न सींधि संवाणी थी,
मूं त तोखे रेशमी वग़ा ऐं सोना
ज़ेवर ड़िना आहिनि,
पर तूं पुराणा, फाटल लटा पाए वेठी आहीं
ईए न समुझ तुंहिंजा अफ़ाल
ड़िसी मां मुड़ी वेंदुसि
तो खे पंहिंजीअ सूंहं जी कशिशि
जी ज़ाण नाहे,
मुंहिंजी जुवानी तो लाए तड़िफी आहे,
मां बेशक़ तो सां ज़ोरु ज़बरदस्ती

करे सघां हा,
पर जेसि तांई तूं मुंहिंजी मुहबत ऐं,
ऐशो इशिरत कुबूलु न कंदीअ
तेसि तांई मुंहिंजी ज़िंदगी फिकी आहे
बियूं औरतूं त खुशि थी
हीउ ताम ऐं सौग़ातूं कुबूलु कंदियूं,
जे तूं आज़ादु थी ई सघीं थी
त पोइ एड़ी ज़िदी छो आहीं?

मारुई

ओ बेरहम बादशाह, तू कहिड़ीअ
आज़ादीअ जी ग़ाल्ह थो करीं?
मां हिन नंढे कमरे में क़ैदि आहियां
जिति ड़ींहं डिठे जो ऊंदहि आहे
छो त सिजु उभिरे ज़रूर थो
पर हिते त ऊंदह ई आहे
तुंहिंजा महकंदड़ि बाग़ बग़ीचा
मुंहिंजे कहिड़े कम जा?
मुंहिंज लाए इहे बेरंगु आहिनि
छो त हिति मुंहिंजा मारू नाहिनि
तूं केतिरी बि आज़माइशि करि
मूंखे टोड़ण जी
पर मां मज़बूत रहंदसि,
मलीर जूं यादिगिरियूं मुंहिंजे
मन में ताज़ियूं आहिनि,
ऐं जेसीं मां मलीरु वरी न
ड़िसंदसि तेसीं बेचैन रहंदियस

उहो ड़ींहु जल्दु ईदो जड़िहं,
तू मूंखे मलीरु वञणु ड़ींदे,
जिति मारू मुंहिंजे इन्तज़ार में आहिनि,
ऐं हा दुनिया सिर्फ़ अंधियारी नाहे,
छो त थर में मुंहिंजे ग़ोठ जे
ब़नीअ में मोती चिमकंदा आहिनि,
तूं चाहे कुझु बि करि उमर
पर मां झुकण वारी नाहियां,
मुंहिंजे जीवन में हिन बेदर्द
क़िले में रहण जी का कशिशि नाहे
असांजे खेत जो हारी फोगसेनु
त वड़ो ग़दारु साबित थियो,
मूंखे हासिलु कीन करे सघियो,
त तो वटि घिड़ी आयो,
मूंखे डुखु पहुचाइण जी नीयत सां
अहिड़ी छा तुंहिंजे कन में
भुणि भुणि कयाईं?
तो खे गुमराह कयाईं ऐं
तूं छा ऐड़ो अब़ोझ आहीं?
जो हुन जे चवण ते
उठ ते चढ़ी मलीरु काहे आएं,
अहिड़ी का जुजिकी लगि़ए जो
मुसाफ़िरु बणिजी मूंखे ज़बरदस्ती
मुंहिंजनि मारूअड़नि खां जुदा कयइ,
तुंहिंजे उठ जे खुड़ियुनि इन्हीअ
जुल्मु ते वारीअ जो तूफ़ान उभारियो.
मुंहिंजियूं अखियूं भरिजी आयूं

पर ग़ोढ़ा रुकिजी विया.
ओ राजा! मुंहिंजी तोखे निमाणी
वेनिती आहे,
जे मां हिति मरां
त मुंहिंजो मुअलु सरीर मलीर में मोकिलिजि
जीअं मां मारूअनि खां मोकिलाइ सघां,
आख़िरी वक़्त में त हर को घर ड़ांहुं वेंदो आहे.

उमर
तूं हिति क़ैदी न आहीं,
तो जहिड़े सुहिणे महिमान जी
महल में आजियां आहे,
मूं तो खे पंहिंजो बणाइण जी,
बेअंत कोशिशि कई
पर नाकामु रहियुसि.
सचुपचु इन्हीअ करे
मुंहिंजीअ आत्मा खे धधिको लग़ो आहे.
एतिरनि वर्हियनि में तोखे
पंहिंजो बणाए न सघियुसि
पर मुंहिंजी हुब वधंदी रही,
हिक तूं ई आहीं जिहं खे
मूं दिलि जानि सां पाइणु चाहियो.
तो जहिड़ी वस में करण जी
सघ बिए कहिं में न आहे.
तूं सभिनी ते पंहिंजीअ सुठाईअ
ऐं सादगीअ जो रंगु चाढ़ी थी
फ़क़्त पंहिंजी सूंहं न पर,

पाकीज़गीअ सां पिणि,
जेतोणिक तो मुंहिंजे प्यारु खे धिकारियो
पर तो मूंखे मोड़ियो आहे,
अजु हिकु राजु पधिरो थो करियां,
मूं पहिरीं त मुंहुं कोन ड्रिनो
नज़रअंदाजु करण चाहियो
पर सीनो टुटो ऐं दिलि बुड़ी

मारूई

अहिड़ी छा ग़ालिह आहे,
उमर तूं व्याकुलु थो लग्गीं?

उमर

कुझु ड्रींहं अगु हिक औरत
मूं वटि आई,
हुन हिक कहाणी बुधाई,
जंहिं ते मां विश्वास नथो करे सघां.
त तुंहिंजे कुटुंब खे सुञणीदी हुई
ऐं मुंहिंजे कुटुंब खे बि
जे इहो वाक़ियो सचो आहे
त मुंहिंजे लाए दुखभरियो आहे,
मूं पंहिंजे दिलि ऐं दिमाग़
मां इहो वाक़ियो विसारणु चाहियो
पर दिलि ई दिलि में ख़बर हुई
त ग़लती थो करियां
त बि मूं तो खे पंहिंजो बणाइण जी कोशिशि कई
मुंहिंजी भुल हुई, पर तो खां जुदा कीअं थियां?

तुंहिंजे पके इरादे असां ब्रिन्ही खे बचायो,
ऐं हाणे मां तोखे हिफ़ाज़त सां
तुंहिंजे घरु मलीर में पहुचाईंदुसि,
हक़ीक़त इहा आहे मारुई
जड़हिं मां पींघे में हुयुसि
मुंहिंजा माइट मलीरु विया हुआ
तुंहिंजीअ माउ मूं खे पंहिंजीअ
थणु मां खीरु पियारियो हुओ,
मां बुख में बेज़ारु हुयिसु
ऐं मुंहिंजीअ माउ जी थण सुकियल हुई,
माड़ोइअ मूंखे पंहिंजी थणु ड़िनी,
मारुई तूं मुंहिंजी भेणु वांगुरु आहीं,
मां पंहिंजी ग़लती सुधारींदुसि,
मूं जेको पापु कयो आहे ऐं
हीउ माहौल घड़ियो आहे,
मूंखे हठु हुओ
त तोखे ख़रीद कंदुसि

मां अञा बि तो सां प्यारु करियां थो,
पर हिक अलग़ि पाकु प्यार जो जज़्बो आहे,
मूं पंहिंजो माणिहूं तुंहिंजे
माइटनि ड्रांहु मोकिलियो आहे
जो मुंहिंजा नियापो ड़ींदुनि,
शाल हू मुंहिंजी माफ़ी क़ुबूलु कनि

मारुई
उमर सूमरा, इहो सभु छा सचु आहे?
त हलु हाणे ई हलूं मलीर डे!

मां पंहिंजनि माइटनि खे ड्रिसां,
ऐं जहिं सां विहांउ थियणो आहे
उन्हीअ सज़ण खे पसां,
छो त मां खेतसेन सां ई
नींहुं निबाहींदसि,
मां हिकु पलु बि इन्तज़ार नथी करे सघां
मारूअड़नि सां मिलण लाए,

उमर

हलु त हलूं, मुंहिंजो उठु बीठो आहे,
तुंहिंजे वञण जो मूंखे ड्राढो दुख आहे,
अचु भेण, मोटी मलीर हलूं,
मुंहिंजी दिलि तो लाए सदाईं सिकंदी
पर मां गुनहगारु नथो बणिजणु चाहियां,

मारुई

ओ राजा, सदाईं आबादु रहीं,
दुआ अथेई,
मूंखे मलीरु मोकिलीं थो,
तो लाए सचु ग़ाल्हाइणु
केड्रो त डुखियो हूंदो,
पर अजु तो मुंहिंजो प्यारु पातो
ऐं साबितु थियो त ईश्वर असां सां आहे.
हलु, जल्दु निकिरूं,
रिणु मूंखे सड़े रहिया आहे
जे देरि कंदासीं, त सिजु न लहे,
ऊंदहि न थिए

उमर

मूंखे हिक चिंता मन में खाए थी,
तुंहिंजी बिरादरी तो ते शकु त न कंदी?
त तूं अपवित्र आहीं,
भगि़वानु न करे त ईएं थिए,
पर जे थियो त मोटी मुंहिंजे
घर अचि जइं,
इहा ख़ातिरी मां तो खे ड़ियां थो,
पर पंहिंजी फ़ौज ज़रूर मलीरु मोकिलींदुसि,
तुंहिंजीअ निगहबानीअ लाए

मारुई

तुंहिंजो पहिरोयों पापु
मूंखे खणण जो,
ऐं हाणे गड्डोगड्डि ताक़त जो इज़िहारु,
वञु राजा तूं मोटी वञु,
मूंखे मलीर नज़र अचे थो,
इन्हीअ धरतीअ में मुंहिंजी हस्ती आहे,
जे हुननि मूं ते भरिवसो न कयो
त मां गर्म शीख़ झलींदसि
हुननि खे साबिती ड़ियण लाए
त मुंहिंजी वागु़ ईश्वर हथि आहे,
ऐं हुननि खे सुधि त पवे
मुंहिंजो सरीरु ऐं आत्मा ब़ुई ,
पाकु आहिनि.

उमर

त हलु मारुई, शाल फ़रिशिता तो सां
ग़ड हुजनि,
पंहिंजी दुनिया में वञु
जिति घटि माणिहूं तो वांगुरु
वतन सां नींहुं लग़ाईंदा आहिनि,
जे हू तुंहिंजी अगनी परीखया
वठनि,
त तूं मूंखे यादि कजाइं
मां पाण परीखया
ड्रियण लाए तयारु रहंदुसि
पाण खे सचो साबितु कंदुसि

ऐं जड़िहिं शक जी वारी
घाटी ऐं तेजु मलीर में उड़ामे,
मारुई ऐं उमर गर्म शीख़
खे हथनि में झलियो
पर शीख़ त हुननि लाए
थधी बर्फ़ जीआं हुई.
ब़ई हिन परखिया मां सलामत
ब़ाहिरि निकिता छो त
ब़ई पाकु हुआ,
इहा बाहि त हू सवलाईअ
सां सही सघिया,
हाणे सग़ा माइट मारुईअ जो
इहो सचु बुधण ऐं समुझण लग़ा,

हुआ त हू असुलु सादा माणिहूं,
असां सभु पंहिंजीअ जन्म भूमीअ
जा ख़ासि आहियूं
ऐं जे राह भुलिजी पऊं
त मोटी इन्हीअ धरतीअ
जे सुर्ग में वञू,

मुरली, आलाप ऐं वण
हिकु थी वेंदा
उतेई असांजो सचो घरु बणजंदो

وٽ هيٺان مُرليءَ جو آلاپ

مارئي

ڪيترا ورهيہ گذريا
پنهنجو رڻ پٽ ڏني،
جادوئي ملير، جڏ واريءَ تي سُرڳ،
عمر سومرا تو مون کان منهنجا
مائٽ ڇنيا
جيڪي مون کي ڏاڍو پيار ڪندا هئا،
پنوهار قبيلي جا مڻڙا مارُو
منهنجي حفاظت ڪميءَ جيئان ڪندا هئا،
تو مون تي ظالمباز
جيئان جهٽ هڻيو ءِ
پنهنجو شڪار بڻايو،
پنهنجي قلعي ۾ قيد ڪيو
مون تي حڪم هلائڻ چاهيو
پر راجا، اِها ڳالھ
تہ طئہ آهي
مان تنهنجي هرگز نہ ٿيندس
چو جو منهنجي دل ٿر ۾
سمايل آهي،
منهنجن ماءُ پيءُ وٽ آهي،
پالٽي ۽ ماڏوئي مون کي
جنم ڏنو،

۽ مان واپس وري ڪيتسين جي
ڪنوار بٽجڻ لاءِ آتي آهيان.

عمر

تون انمول ۽ هنيلي نار آهين
جنهن کي مان پائڻ ٿو چاهيان،
جنهن ملڪ ۾ تنهنجي دل لڳي آهي
اُتي توکي سيني وساريو آهي
جي تون موٽي ويندين ت هو
توتي ننولي ڪندا،
توکي مهٽا ڏيندا،
هو سمجهندا
تون اپوتر ٿي چڪي آهين،
توکي نندو ڀار ڪري نه ليکيندا،
تنهن ڪري تتل واريءَ جي تات چڏ
۽ منهنجو چيو مڃُ
مان توسان بيحد محبت ڪيان ٿو،
تون ئي مون کي خوش ڪري سگهين ٿي.
پر تنهنجي لاءِ ت مان ڪو
دشمن آهيان،
ايتري ذن دؤلت هجڻ باوجود،
مون تنهنجو هٿ جهلڻ چاهيو،
جيئن هيءَ ملڪيت توسان ونڊيان
مان تو سان سڻو ورتاءُ ڪيان ٿو،

ءُ اُميد ت مان تنهنجي چُڳي
موٽ جي لائق آهيان.

مارئي

تنهنجي لاءِ مليرُ ٿر جي رڄ هوندو،
پر منهنجي لاءِ سارو جهان آهي،
مان ڀل ڪوهين پري آهيان
پر اُهو ڳوٺ مون کي پيارو آهي،
جت مون پاڻ کي مُڪمل يانئيو آهي،
حالانڪ ورهيہ لنگهي ويا
پر منهنجو روح اڃ ڀڳ زنده آهي.
منهنجن ماروئرن شايد مون کي وساريو هوندو
پر منهنجيءَ دل ۾ هو سدا رهندا،
تنهنجي سرد قلعي جي ديوارن،
ڪان وڌيڪ عزيز رهندا
جتي تون درٻار لڳائيندو آهين
تون ڀل راجا آهين پر مان
تنهنجي راند لاءِ رانديڪو ناهيان،
اِنهيءَ غلطفهميءَ ۾ نہ رهجانءِ
تہ مان توسان ڪڏهن وهانءُ ڪندس.

عمر

تون پاڻ کي بدشڪل ٻڌائڻ
جي ڪوشش ڪرين ٿي،

نَ ڪِ وار ڏوئي نَہ سينڌ سنواري ٿي،
مون تہ توکي ريشمي وڳا ۽ سونا
زيور ڏِنا آهن،
پر تون پُراٽا، قاتل لٽا پائي ويٺي آهين،
ائين نَہ سمجھہ تہ تنهنجا افال
ڏسي مان مُڙي ويندُس،
تو کي پنهنجيءَ سونهن جي ڪشش
جي ڄاڻ ناهي،
منهنجي جواني تو لاءِ ترسي آهي،
مان بيشڪ توسان زور زبردستي
ڪري سگھان هان،
پر جيستائين تون منهنجي محبت ۽
عيشو اِشرت قبول نہ ڪندين،
تيستائين منهنجي زندگي ڦڪي آهي
ڀيون عورتون تہ خوش ٿي
هيءُ طعام ۽ سوغاتون قبول ڪنديون،
جي تون آزاد ٿي ئي سگھين ٿي،
تہ پوءِ ايڏي ضدي ڇو آهين؟

مارئي

او بي رحم بادشاهہ، تون ڪهڙيءَ
آزاديءَ جي ڳالھہ تو ڪرين؟
مان هن ننڍي ڪمري ۾ قيد آهيان
جت ڏينهن ڏئي جو اونڌہ آهي

چو تہ سج اُپري ضرور تو
پر هتي تہ اوندهہ ئي آهي
تنهنجا مهكندڙ باغ بغيچا
منهنجي كهڙي كر جا؟
منهنجي لاءِ اِهي بي رنگ آهن
چو تہ منهنجا مارون ناهن.
تون كيتري بہ آزمائش كر
مون كي ٽوڙڻ جي
پر مانمضبوط رهندس،
ملير جون يادگريون منهنجي
من ۾ تازيون آهن،
۽ جيسين مان ملير وري نہ
ڏسندس تيسين بيچئن رهنديس.
اُهو ڏينهن جلد ايندو جڏهن
تون مون كي ملير وجڻ ڏيندين،
جت مارُون منهنجي اِنتظار ۾ آهن،
۽ ها دنيا صرف انڌياري ناهي،
چو تہ ٿر ۾ منهنجي ڳوٺ جي
بنيءَ ۾ موتي چمكندا آهن،
تون چاهي كجهہ بہ كر عمر
پر مان جهكڻ واري ناهيان،
منهنجي جيون ۾ هن بي درد
قلعي ۾ رهڻ جي كا كشش ناهي.
اسان جي كيت جو هاري قوگسين

تہ وڏو غدار ثابت ٿيو،

مون کي حاصل ڪين ڪري سگهيو،

تہ تو وٽ گهڙي آيو،

مون کي ڏک پهچائڻ جي نيت سان

اهڙي تنهنجي ڪن ۾

چا پِٽ پِٽ ڪيائين؟

توکي گمراه ڪيائين، ۽

تون چا ايڏو اڀوجھ آهين؟

جو هُن جي چوٽ تي

اُٺ تي چڙهي ملير ڪاهي آئين،

اهڙي ڪا جهجهڪي لِگئہ جو

مسافر بٽجي مون کي زبردستي

ماروئڙن کان جدا ڪيئہ،

تنهنجي اُٺ جي ڪڙين اِنهيءَ

ظلم تي واريءَ جو طوفان اُٿاريو.

منهنجيون اکيون پِرجي آيون

پر ڳوڙها رڪجي ويا.

او راجا! منهنجي توکي نماڻي

وينتي آهي،

جي مان هت مران

تہ منهنجو مئل سرير ملير ۾ موڪلج،

جيئن مان ماروئڙن کان موڪلائي سگهان،

آخري وقت ۾ تہ هر ڪو گهر ڏانهن ويندو آهي.

عمر

تون هت قيدي نہ آهين،

تو جهڙي سهڻي مهمان جي

محل ۾ آجيان آهي،

مون توکي پنهنجو بٽائڻ جي

بي انت ڪوشش ڪئي

پر ناڪام رهيَس.

سچ پچ اِنهيءَ ڪري

منهنجيءَ آتما کي ڏاڍو لڳو آهي.

ايترن ورهين ۾ توکي

پنهنجو بٽائي نہ سگهيُس

پر منهنجي حُب وڌندي رهي،

هڪ تون ئي آهين جنهن کي

مون دل جان سان پائڻ چاهيو.

تو جهڙي وس ۾ ڪرڻ جي

سگهہ ٻئي ڪنهن کي بہ ناهي.

تون سيني تي پنهنجي سنائيءَ

ءِ سادگيءَ جو رنگ چاڙهين ٿي

فقط پنهنجي سونهن نہ پر

پاڪيزگي ئي سان پڻ،

جيتوڻيڪ تو منهنجي پيار کي ڏڪاريو

پر تو مون کي موڙيو آهي،

اڄ هڪ راز پڌرو ٿو ڪريان،

مون ڦرين تہ منهن کون نہ ڏنو،

نظرانداز ڪرڻ چاھيو
پر سينو ٿِئو ۽ دل ٻڌي،

مارئي
اھڙي ڇا ڳالھ آھي؟
عمر تون وياڪل ٿو لڳين

عمر
ڪجھ ڏينھن اڳ ھڪ عورت
مون وٽ آئي،
ھن ھڪ ڪھاڻي ٻڌائي
جنھن تي مان وشواس نٿو ڪري سگھان.
ت تنھنجي ڪٽنب ڪي سجاٽيندي ھئي
۽ منھنجي ڪٽنب ڪي ب
جي اِھو واقعو سچ آھي
ت منھنجي لاءِ ڏڪ پريو آھي،
مون پنھنجي دل ۽ دماغ
مان اِھو واقعو وسارڻ چاھيو،
پر دل ئي دل ۾ خبر ھئي
ت غلطي ٿو ڪريان
ت ب مون توڪي پنھنجو بٽائڻ جي ڪوشش ڪئي،
منھنجي پُل ھئي، پر تو ڪان جدا ڪيئن ٿيان؟
تنھنجي پڪي اِرادي اسان ٻنھي ڪي بچايو،
۽ ھاڻي مان توڪي حفاظت سان

تنهنجي گهر ملير ۾ پهچائيندس،
حقيقت اِها آهي مارئي
جڏهن مان پينگهي ۾ هُيس،
منهنجا مائٽ ملير ويا هئا
تنهنجيءَ ماءُ مون کي پنهنجيءَ
ٽِج مان کير پياريو هئو،
مان بک ۾ بيزار هيس،
۽ منهنجي ماءُ جي ٽِج سُکيل هئي،
ماڏوئيءُ مونکي پنهنجي ٽِج ڏني،
مارئي تون منهنجي پيٽ وانگر آهين،
مان پنهنجي غلطي سُداريندس،
مون جيڪو پاپ ڪيو آهي ۽
هيءُ ماحول گهٽِيو آهي،
مون کي هٺ هئو
ت توکيخريد ڪندس،

مان اجا ب تو سان پيار ڪريان تو،
پر هڪ الڳ پاڪ پيار جو جذبو آهي،
مون پنهنجو ماٺهو تنهنجي
مائٽن ڏانهن موڪليو آهي
جو منهنجو نياپو ڏيندُن،
شال هو منهنجي معافي قبول ڪن.

مارئي

عمر سومرا، اِهو سپ چا سچ آهي؟
تہ هل هاٹي ئي هلون ملير ڏي!
مان پنهنجن مائٽن کي ڏسان،
۽ جنهن سان وهانءُ ٿيٽو آهي
أنهيءَ سجڻ کي پسان
چو تہ مان کيتسين سان ئي
نينهن نيائيندس،
مان هڪ پل بہ اِنتظار نٿي ڪري سگهان
ماروئڙن سان ملڻ لاءِ.

عمر

هل تہ هلون، منهنجو اُٽ بيٺو آهي،
تنهنجي وڃڻ جو مونکي ڏاڍو ڏک آهي،
اڇ پيڻ، موٺي ملير هلون،
منهنجي دل تو لاءِ سدائين سڪندي
پر مان گنهگار نٿو بٽجڻ چاهيان.

مارئي

او راجا! سدائين آباد رهين،
دعا اٿيئي،
مونکي ملير موڪلين ٿو،
تو لاءِ سچ ڳالهائڻ
ڪيڏو تہ ڏکيو هوندو،

پر اڄ تو منهنجو پيار پاتو،
۽ ثابت ٿيو تہ ايشور اسان سان آهي
هل، جلد، نڪرون،
رٿ مونکي سڌي رهيو آهي.
جي دير ڪنداسين،
تہ سج نہ لهي، اوندھ نہ ٿئي،

عمر

مون ڪي هڪ چنتا من ۾ ڪائي ٿي،
تنهنجي برادري تو تي شڪ تہ نہ ڪندي؟
تہ تون اپوتر آهين.
پڳوان نہ ڪري تہ ائين ٿئي،
پر جي ٿيو تہ موٽي منهنجي
گھر اچجانءِ.
اِها خاطري مان توکي ڏيان ٿو،
پر پنهنجي فوج ضرور ملير
موڪليندس
تنهنجي نگھبانيءَ لاءِ

مارئي

تنهنجو پهريو نپاپ
مون ڪي ڪٽڻ جو،
۽ هاڻي گڏوگڏ طاقت جو اِظهار،
وڃ راجا تون موٽي وڃ،

مون کي ملير نظر اچي ٿو،
اِنهيءَ ڌرتيءَ هر منهنجي هستي آهي،
جي هنن مون تي پروسو نہ ڪيو
تہ مان گرم شيخ جھليندس
هنن کي
ثابتيڙين لاءِ
تہ منهنجي واڳ ايشور هٿ آهي،
۽ هنن کي سڌ پوي تہ
منهنجو سرير ۽ آتما ٻئي
پاڪ آهن.

عمر
تہ هل مارئي، شال فرشتا تو سان
گڏ هجن،
پنهنجي دنيا هر وچ،
جتگھٽ ماٺو
تو وانگر
وطن سان نينهن لڳائيندا آهن،
جي هوُ تنهنجي اڳني پريکيا وٺن،
تہ تون مون کي بہ ياد ڪجانءِ
مان پاڻ پريکيا ڏيڻ لاءِ تيار رهندس،
پاڻ کي سچو ثابت ڪندس.

ءِ جڏھن شڪ جي واري
گھاني ءِ تيز مليير مِ اُڏامي،
مارئي ءِ عمر گرم شيخ
ڪي هٿ مِ جھليو
پر شيخ تہ هنن لاءِ
تَلدي برف جيئان هئي.
هئي هن پريڪيا مان سلامت
ٻاهر نڪتا چو تہ
هئي پاڪُ هئا،
اِها باھ تہ هوُ سولائيءَ
سان سھي سگھيا،
هاٽي سگا مائٽ مارئيءَ جو
اِهو سچ بَدڪ ءِ سمجھڻ لڳا،
هئا تہ هوُ اصل سادا ماڻھو،
اسان سڀ پنهنجيءَ جنم يومي ءَ
جا خاص آهيون،
ءِ جي راھ پلجي پئون
تہ موٽي اِنهيءَ قرتيءَ
جي سُرڳ مِ وجون،

مُرلي، آلاپ ءِ وَٽ
هڪُ ٿي ويندا
اُتي ئي اسان جو سچو گھر ٻَجندو.

Diamonds and Coal

Discard your former ways, be free
from all you learnt before.
Humility's scarf around your neck
do wear ... with poverty.

Diamonds and Coal

Leela
What is coal
and what is diamond
is for the earth to decide
in the stillness of its core
when heat and light coalesce silently
or in a rumbling, heaving roar.
I sank into the depths and confused
the difference between the two
and when I came up for air,
I found I had lost to you.
In one crazed instant, my eye
had fallen on your *nau lakh haar*
I lost my sense and sanity,
left the door to my love ajar
and faith crept out
like a mouse into the night,
so silently it vanished,
in the shadow of candlelight.
I have spent so many years
as King Chanesar's special bride.
I could not imagine another life
where I would not be by his side.
What a mistake I made
when, for an instant, I could not tell
the difference between my true treasure
and these diamonds that came from hell.
Your *nau lakh haar* is just *koyla*
that chokes my bitter throat
I gave him up to you for this,

and he is now so remote.
I have lost it all, the life I led,
for a moment's petty greed
And I have learned the only truth –
that my king is all I need.

Kounru
But he is no longer yours, dear Leela.
I fought for him and won.
It took me a long while to claim my reward,
and prove that I was someone
who could make this man so happy
and not miss the years he spent with you.
You valued him less than a necklace.
What else did you think he would do?
For a man's pride is what counts most to him
and you thought diamonds mattered more.
Chanesar will never return to you;
of this, you can be sure.

I have journeyed far from Lakhpat,
where princes sought me from across the land
But my father, King Khangar, knew
I wanted no one else's hand
except the one whom every woman cherished,
the Dasro King of Debal,
a powerful, handsome monarch
who held me in his thrall.
But I was told I could never have him
for he belonged to you,
his childhood sweetheart, who knew him well,
whose love for him was true.
And then, when I arrived

in a rich merchant's disguise,
my mother Murki accompanying me
to help me win my prize,
you did not think to ask where we had come from
and Jakhro never told you,
though he, your trusted minister,
was the only one who knew
the truth beneath my tradesman's garb,
the fact that I was there
to claim Chanesar as my own,
a man beyond compare.

Leela
Jakhro brought you to me as a servant maid
and I thought I was helping you.
You seemed in need of money.
I did not imagine you were untrue.
I pitied your circumstances,
believing the ragged clothes you wore.
You said you wanted to serve me;
I opened my palace door.
Your mother was an expert weaver, you said,
and you could keep a house well.
You were right, you kept my house;
in this, you did excel!
When I found you crying
in the chamber of my king,
I did not know it was because
you wanted my husband's ring.
Your tears, you said, were only because
you once had wealth and lost it.
I was foolish to believe you;
I let my boundary down; you crossed it.

You told me of your diamond necklace,
said it was all that remained of your riches
and you offered it to me in exchange for my man –
one night, that's all, you both said – you witches!
I was blinded by the dazzle of the diamonds,
let you into my husband's bed,
persuaded him to accept you,
just for a few hours, I said.
I did not think it would matter
for there had been other women too.
I thought no woman could take him from me,
and certainly not a woman like you.
All the women in my husband's harem,
not one had comparable charm.
So many have shared his bed;
I saw no cause for alarm.
But you – you damaged what was dear to me
and did me so much harm!

Kounru

You grew complacent in your lover's arms,
a mistake no woman should make,
and because you were so unwise,
he became mine to take.
How cheap you made your marriage,
exchanging it for ornaments!
How could you think when he found out
that the monarch would relent
and forgive you for your foolish choice,
your momentary greed?
I gave you a precious necklace
and it helped me to succeed.
I conquered the place

that once belonged to you,
I worked hard for this position,
and you did not have a clue.
Though I was no servant maid
I left my own palace to clean your floors.
I knew that this humility
would open all the doors.
Now Chanesar is mine
and you will pay the price.
I hope these dazzling gems you wear
will instead suffice.

Leela

This diamond necklace is no comfort to me,
now back in my parents' home,
and those who used to envy me
hurl taunts wherever I roam.
Your scheme may have succeeded,
but I will win my husband back.
for we have spent years together
and he knows I have the knack
of understanding his innermost thoughts.
I will make him forget you soon.
He, too, had made a mistake that night
in that drunken moment of doom.
You and your conniving mother arranged
for a priest to marry you both.
knowing he was not in his senses,
you made him take an oath
that I know he regretted in the morning
when he realised what you had done.
He was angry with me, but his fury
was not directed at me alone.

For you cheated, not just me,
but the man you claim to love as well,
and though at that unfortunate moment
Chanesar accepted your stratagem,
he will return to the one he's loved
and it is you he will condemn.

And Leela, who had lost her love,
though years had passed, stayed true to him.
Full of regret, she could not forget
the man she had lost on a whim.
So when Jakhro asked her help
to marry a lovely girl from Leela's land
she agreed to make it possible
for Jakhro to gain her hand
but on the condition that he, in turn,
bring Chanesar back to her;
The wedding would be the perfect time
to return to the way they were.
So Jakhro begged the King to honour him
and attend the ceremony.
The King was reluctant but could not refuse
his trusted Jakhro's plea
and at the nuptials, the veiled singer before him
sang a haunting song of immeasurable loss and grief
It stirred memories of a woman he once loved;
he, too, began to weep.
But the graceful woman with the koel's tongue
could surely soothe the pain,
so he commanded she show her face
and was dumbstruck, seeing Leela again.

To this day, Leela and Chanesar lie
in an eternal embrace
as heat and light coalesce silently
in the deepest submerged space
and beneath a mantle of glowing rock
in the cracked earth's inner core
Leela creates her own diamonds
from the crystal tears that fell before,
and these were the most valuable of all.

हीरा ऐं कोइला

लीला

कोइलो छा?
हीरो छा?
इहो फ़ैसलो त धरती ई कंदी
पंहिंजे ख़ामोश गर्भ में
जड़िहं तपत ऐं रोशनीअ जो
ख़ामोश मेलाप थिए,
या वरी बाहि जा शोला कड़कनि गर्जनि,
मां उन्हीअ बुड़तर में,
बिन्हीं जे विच में फ़रक़ु करण
में मुंझियुसि,

जड़िहं होश आयो, मूं साहु खंयो
चिटीअ तरह समुझियो त
मूं हारायो,
बसि हिक नज़र तुंहिंजे नउलखे
हार ते पेई
मुंहिंजी दिल सुरिकी
हार जी ख़ूबसूरतीअ त मुंहिंजियूं
मतियूं ई मारे छड़ियूं,
इन्हीअ आंधि मांधि में दरु खुलियलु रखी
मां ख़ामोश हली वियसि... ऊंदहि मां,
पाण खे अंधकार में धिको डिनुमि
मूं सां गडु ग़ाइबु थियो विश्वासु

जो मेण बतीअ जे पाछे में
मूं कएं वरिह्य गुज़ारिया आहिनि
राजा चनेसर जी पट राणी बणिजी
राजा खां सवाइ जीवन जी
कल्पना कई कान हुई
मां हुन सां गडु कान हूंदिस
मूं केड़ी न वड़ी चुक कई,
हिक कमज़ोर खिन में
मां पंहिंजे असुली ख़ज़ाने ऐं
अजायनि हीरनि में तफ़ावतु
न ज़ाणे सधियसि
तुंहिंजो नउलखो हारु त कोइले
जे मुल्ह वारो आहे, पत्थरु आहे,
जेको मुंहिंजे लाइ फाहो थी पियो आहे,
मूं पंहिंजो प्यारो पिरीं
हिक ख़सीस हार लाइ तोखे
डिनो ऐं हू हाणे मूंखां
दूरि आहे,
मुंहिंजी अजाई लालच
मूं खे ड़ाढी भारी पेई,
मूं सभु कुझु विञायो
मूं सचो सबकु सिखियो
मूंखे मुंहिंजे राजा खां
सवाइ बियो कुझु बि न घुरिजे.

कोनरू

पर प्यारी लीला, हाणे हू तुंहिंजो नाहे,
मूं हुन खे ज़ोरीअ हासिलु कयो आहे,

मूंखे थोरो वक़्त लग्ो
पंहिंजो इनाम हासिलु करण लाए
पंहिंजो पाणु साबितु करण लाए
कि मां हिक राजा खे ख़ुशि
करण जे लाइक़ ज़रूर आहियां
एड्ो ख़ुशि कयो हुन खे
जो तो सां गुज़िरियल वरिह्ा
हू विसारे वेठो,
तो त राजा जो क़दुरु
हार खां बि घटि कयो,
तोखे छा लग्ो, हू छा कंदो?
हिक मर्द लाइ संदसि मानु
सभ खां वड्ो आहे,
तुंहिंजे लेखे हीरा अहम आहिनि,
मूंखे पक आहे त चनेसर
तो वटि असुलु मोटी कीन ईंदो
मूं लखपत मां सफ़रु कयो आहे
हर राज़ में जिति कएं राजकुमार,
मूं लाए आता हुआ,
पर मुंहिंजो पीउ राजा खंघरु ज़ुणींदो
हुओ त हिकु ई राजा
मुंहिंजे दिलि में वसियो पिए
औरतूं जंहिं ते मोहित हुयूं... उहो हो
देवल सूबे जो दासिरो राजा चनेसरु,
ठाहूको ऐं ताकतवर बादशाह
जंहिं मूंखे मोहियो हो.

मूं खे सभिनी बुधायो
त चनेसर तुंहिंजो नंढिपिणि जो
प्रेमी आहे ऐं मुंहिंजो कड़हिं न थींदो
छो जो तूं राजा खे
सचो प्यार कंदी आहीं
मां हिक अमीर वापारीअ
जे वेस में पंहिंजी माउ मुर्कीअ सां
गडु हिति आयसि
पंहिंजे प्यार खे पाइण लाए
तो त अखियूं बंदि करे बिना
कंहिं पुछा ग़ाछा जे असां खे
महल में कमु ड़िनो,
तुंहिंजो विश्वास जोग़ी वज़ीरु जाखीरो
पिणि चुपि रहियो,
जेतोणीक तुंहिंजे भरवसे वारे
वज़ीर खे सज़ी ख़बर हुई
त मां वेसु मटाए, वापारी बणिजी
हिति छो आई हुयसि,

चनेसर पंहिंजे दिलि जे राजा खे
हासिलु करण लाइ,
अहिड़ो राजा जंहिंजी कंहिं
सां बि भेट नाहे.

लीला
जाखीरो तोखे मूं वटि
नौकिराणी करे वठी आयो,
मूं तोखे मदद करण चाही,

मूंखे लग़ो त तोखे पैसनि जी ज़रूरत आहे,
मूंखे तुंहिंजीअ हालत
ते क़्यासु आयो,
मूंखे ख़्वाबु ख़्यालु बि कोन
हो त तूं कूड़ी आहीं,
तुंहिंजे फाटलनि कपड़नि ते
विश्वासु कयुमि,
तो त ईअ डेखारी ड़िनो
त मुंहिंजी शेवा कंदींअ
तो चयो तुंहिंजी माउ
उणण में माहिर आहे
तूं घरु सुठो संभालींदी आहीं,
हा तो सचु चयो, मुंहिंजो
घरु तो बहितिरीन संभालियो !
तो त बरबादि करे छड़ियो
जड़िहिं मूं तो खे राजा
जे कमरे में रूअंदो ड़िठो
तड़िहिं मूं अयाणीअ खे
ख़बर कान हुई त तुंहिंजी
नज़र राजा जी मुंडीअ ते आहे,
तो त वरी कूड़ ग़ाल्हाए,
नकुली ग़ोड़हा ग़ारे चयो
तूं पंहिंजनि सुठनि ड़ींहनि खे
यादि करे रोई रही आहें
मां बेअकुलु हुयसि जो तो
ते भरविसो कयुमि,
मूं पाण सां पाण ई

जुठि कई ऐं तोखे
हद पारि करण जो मौक़ो ड़िनो,
तो मूंखे पंहिंजे हीरनि जे
हार जी ग़ालिह बुधाई,
तो मूंखे हीरनि जे हार
जी लालच ड़िनी उन
बदिरां मां तो खे पंहिंजे राजा
सां हिक राति गुज़ारण जो शर्तुं रखियो,
बस हिक राति ......
तव्हां बिन्हीं गड़िजी चयो
बस हिक राति ......
मां नादान
तो खे पंहिंजे भतार जी सेजा ते
सुम्हण ड़िनुमि,
मूं राजा खे मिंथूं
कयूं त तो खे क़ुबूल करे
सिर्फ़ कुझु कलाकनि लाइ क़ुबूल करे

मूं भांयो त इहा का वड़ी ग़ालिह नाहे,
छो त राजा जूं बियूं राणियूं बि हुयूं,
मूंखे पाण ते ग़ुरूर ऐं
यक़ीनु हो त काबि छोकिरी
मूं खां राजा खे जुदा न करे सघंदी,
राजा जे ज़नानख़ाने में का बि
औरत न हुई जंहिं जो दीदारु
करे राजा मूं खे विसारे,
केतिरियूं कामिणियूं आयूं वयूं,

मूंखे कड़िहिं बि कंहिं मां
ख़तिरो कोन थियो,
पर तूं... तो छीहो रसायो,
ऐं मूंखे डुखु ड़िनो.

कोनरू

तूं त पंहिंजे पिरींअ जे भाकुर
में समाइजी बेख़ौफ़ थीयं,
इहा ग़लती कंहिं बि औरत
खे न करण घुरिजे,
तुंहिंजीअ नादानीअ करे
मूं राजा खे रीझायो,
तो त पंहिंजीअ शादीअ खे
मज़ाकु समझियो, एड़ो सस्तो बणायो,
जो ज़ेवरनि बदिले राजा ड़िनो !
तो छा सोचियो त राजा खे
जड़िहिं ख़बर पवंदी त हू रहमदिलि थींदो ?
ऐं तुंहिंजीअ बेवकूफ़ीअ खे
मॉफ़ु कंदो ?
तुंहिंजी लालच भुलाए छड़ींदो ?
मूं तो खे हिकु अमोलकु हारु ड़िनो,
ऐं उन्हीअ ज़रीए तुंहिंजे
वर ऐं महल ते सोभ पाती,
इहा जग़ह पाइण लाइ मूं
पाणु पतोड़ियो,
ऐं तो खे पतो बि न पियो,
जेतोणीक मां नौकराणी कान हुयसि

मूं पंहिंजो महलु छडियो
तुंहिंजे महल जो फ़र्शु धोतो,
मूंखे ज़ाण हुई त
हीअ निमाणाई
मुंहिंजे लाइ सभु दर खोलींदी,
हाणे चनेसर फ़क़्त मुंहिंजो आहे
ऐं तो खे क़ीमत चुकाइणी आहे
उमेद त इहे मणिया
जेके तो तन ते सजाया
इहा मटा सटा सही आहे.

लीला

हीउ हीरनि जो हारु
मुंहिंजे जीअ जो जंजालु
मुंहिंजे पेके घर में
जेके मूं ते रशक़ कंदा हुआ,
अजु उहे ई हलंदे चलंदे
मूंखे ज़ोर सां महिणा था ड़ियनि,

तुंहिंजी रिथ शायदि कामियाबु थी हूंदी
पर मां पंहिंजे पिरींअ खे पक पाईंदसि,
छो त असां घणा साल
गडु गुज़ारिया आहिनि,
हू ज़ाणे थो त मां
संदसि हर गालिह ऐं ख़्यालु
समुझंदी आहियां,
मूंखे पक आहे त मां राजा

जे दिलि मां तुंहिंजो नालो
निशानु मिटाईंदिस,
मुंहिंजे चवण ते राजा जल्द ई
तो खे विसारींदो,

उन्हीअ कारी राति
राजा खे नशे जी हालति में आणे
तूं ऐं तुंहिंजी चालाक माउ
गड़िजी साज़िश रची ऐं
पंडितु घुराए तव्हां शादी रचाई,
तव्हां हिन खां ज़बरदस्ती
इंजामु वरितो,

सुबह जो राजा खे पंहिंजीअ
चुक जो अहिसासु थियो
हू ड़ाढो पशेमानु थियो
जड़िहं हुन खे ख़बर पेई
त तो कहिड़ी चालि हली आहे,
हू मूं ते काविड़ियलु हो
पर हुन जी नाराज़गी फ़क़त
मूं सां न हुई छो त तो
सिर्फु मूंखे न ठगियो
पर उन इंसान सां बि
दग़ाबाज़ी कई जंहिं खे तूं
प्यारु कंदी आहीं... इहो कहिड़ो नींहुं ?
जेतोणीक उन हिक पल लाइ
चनेसर तुंहिंजी हरकत क़ुबूल कई

हू ज़रूर मोटी मूं वटि ईंदो
छो त हू मूं सां बेहदि
मोहब्बत कंदो आहे
ऐं तोखे हिक ड़ींहं
ज़रूर धिकारींदो.

वेचारी लीला पंहिंजो पिरीं
विंञायो,
पर प्यार में वफ़ादारु रही
पाण पछितायाईं त हिक पल
जी कमज़ोरीअ करे
प्रीतमु रुसी वियो.
हिक ड़ींहं जाखीरो
लीला खां मदद घुरण आयो,
लीला जे ग़ोठ जी हिक
सुहिणीअ ते जाखीरो
फ़िदा थियो हो
शादी करण पिए चाहियाईं
इन्हीअ करे लीला खां सहारो वठण आयो,
लीला चयुसि त मां तुंहिंजी मदद
ज़रूर कंदसि पर मुंहिंजी हिक
शर्त आहे,
जे तूं चनेसर खे मूं वटि
वठी ईंदें त मां
तुंहिंजी शादी उन
सुहिणीअ सां कराईंदसि.
जाखीरे जी शादीअ में चनेसर

सां गड्जण जी इच्छा लीला
जे मन में उथी.
पोइ जाखीरो लग़ी वियो राजा
खे मज़ाइण में त
हू संदसि शादीअ में शामिलु थिए.
चनेसर जी मर्ज़ी कान हुई
पर जाखीरे जो अर्जु बुधी
खेसि नाकारे न सघियो.
जाखीरे जे विहांउ जे ड्रींहुं
पर्दे में ढकियल गाइका
हिक सोज़ भरियो गीतु
राजा जे साम्हूं पेशि कयो,
राजा बेचैन थियो ऐं
खेसि पंहिंजी पटराणी यादि आई
यादगीरियुनि जे तूफ़ान में
राजा जूं अखियूं भरीजी आयूं,
हिन सुंदिरीअ जे कोयल जियां
मधुर आवाज़ राजा जी कुझु
पीड़ा दूरि कई,
राजा संदसि घूंघट खोलण
जी ख़्वाहिश कई,
लीला खे वरी डिसी,
राजा वाइड़ो थियो.
अजु ड्रींहं ताईं लीला चनेसर
अमरता जे भाकुर में
ब़धल आहिनि,
जींअं तपत ऐं रोशनी

सांत में साथ रहंदा आहिनि,
हिक गहिरीअ बुड्ल ख़ाल में
चिमकंदड़ छिप जे अंदरि
फाटल धरतीअ जे अंदरूनी
हिसे में,
लीला नज़र अचे थी,
लीला पंहिंजनि लुड़कनि मां
पाण हीरा रचे थी,
इहे ई सभ खां अमुल्ह आहिनि.

هيرا ۽ ڪوئلا

ليلا

ڪوئلو ڇا؟

هيرو ڇا؟

اِهو فيصلو تہ ڌرتي ئي ڪندي

پنهنجي خاموش گرڀ ۾

جڏهن تپت ۽ روشنيءَ جو

خاموشيءَ سان ميلاپ ٿئي،

يا وري باھ جا شولا ڪڙڪن گرجن،

مان اُنهي ڀِنتر ۾،

ٻنهي جي وچ ۾ فرق ڪرڻ

۾ منجهيس،

جڏهن هوش آيو، مون ساھ ڪنيو

ڇنيءَ طرح سمجهيو تہ

مون هارايو،

بس هڪ نظر تنهنجي نؤلکي

هار تي پيئي

منهنجي دل سُرڪي

هار جي خوبصورتيءَ تہ منهنجيون

متيون ئي ماري ڇڏيون،

اِنهيءَ آنڌ مانڌ ۾ در ڪليل ڪري

مان خاموش هلي ويس... اوندھ مان،

پاڻ کي انتڪار ۾ ڏڪو ڏنر

۽ مون سان گڏ غائب ٿيو وشواس

جو ميڊبتيءَ جي پاڇي ۾

مون ڪئين ورهيه گذاريا آهن

راجا چنيسر جي پٽ راٽي بڻجي

راجا ڪان سواءِ جيون جي

ڪلپنا ڪئي ڪانه هئي

مان هن سان گڏ نه هوندس

مون ڪيڏي نه وڏي چُڪ ڪئي،

هڪ ڪمزور ڪن ۾

مان پنهنجي اصلي خزاني ۽

اجاين هيرن ۾ تفاوت

نه جاڻي سگهيس

تنهنجو نؤلکو هار ته ڪوئلي

جي ملھ وارو آهي، پٿر آهي،

جيڪو منهنجي لاءِ قاهو تي پيو آهي،

مون پنهنجو پيارو پرين

هڪ خصيص هار لاءِ توکي

ڏنو ۽ هوُ هاڻي مون کان

دوُر آهي،

منهنجي اجائي لالچ

مون کي ڏاڍي ياري پيئي،

مون سڀ ڪجهه وڃايو

مون سچو سبق سکيو

مون ڪي منهنجي راجا ڪان

سواءِ ٻيو ڪجهه ٻه نه گهرجي.

ڪؤنرُو

پر پياري ليلا، ھاڻي ھو تنهنجو ناھي،

مون هُن ڪي زوريءَ حاصل ڪيو آھي،

مون ڪي ٿورو وقت لڳو

پنهنجي اِنعام حاصل ڪرڻ لاءِ

پنهنجو پاڻ ثابت ڪرڻ لاءِ

ڪ مان ھڪ راجا ڪي خوش

ڪرڻ جي لائق ضرور آھيان

ايڏو خوش ڪيو ھن ڪي

جو توسان گذريل ورهيه

ھُو وساري وينو،

تو ته راجا جو قدر

ھار ڪان ٻه گهٽ ڪيو،

تو ڪي چا لڳو، ھُو چا ڪندو؟

ھڪ مرد لاءِ سندس مانُ

سڀ ڪان وڏو آھي،

تنهنجي ليکي ھيرا اهم آھن،

مون ڪي پڪ آھي ته چنيسر

تو وٽ اصل موتي ڪين ايندو

مون لکپت مان سفر ڪيو آھي

ھر راڄ ۾ جت ڪئين راڄڪمار،

مون لاءِ عاطا هئا،

پر منهنجو پيءُ راجا كنگهر ڃاٽيندو

هئو ته هك ئي راجا

منهنجي دل ۾ وسيو پئي

عورتون جنهن تي موهت هيون... اُهو هو

ديول صوبي جو داسرو راجا چنيسر،

ناهوكو ۽ طاقتور بادشاه

جنهن مون كي موهيو هئو.

مون كي سيني ڀڏايو

ته چنيسر تنهنجو ننڊپڻ جو

پريمي آهي ۽ منهنجو كڏهن نه ٽيندو

چو جو تون راجا كي

سچو پيار كندي آهين

مان هك امير واپاريءَ

جي ويس ۾ پنهنجي ماءُ مُركيءَ سان

گڏ هت آيس

پنهنجي پيار كي پائڻ لاءِ

تو ته اكيون بند كري بنا

كنهن پيا ڳاڃا جي اسان كي

محل ۾ كر ڏنو،

تنهنجو وشواس جوڳي وزيرجاكيرو

ڀڻ چپ رهيو،

جيتوٽيڪ تنهنجي پروسي واري
وزير ڪي سڄي خبر هئي
ته مان ويس مٽائي، واپاري بڻجي
هت چو آئي هيس،

چنيسر پنهنجي دل جي راجا ڪي
حاصل ڪرڻ لاءِ،
اهڙو راجا جنهن جي ڪنهن
سان به پيٽ ناهي.

ليلا

جاڪيرو توڪي مون وٽ
نوڪرياڻي ڪري وٺي آيو،
مون تو ڪي مدد ڪرڻ چاهي،
مون ڪي لڳو ته تو ڪي پئسن
جي ضرورت آهي،
مون ڪي تنهنجيءَ حالت
تي قياس آيو،
مون ڪي خواب خيال به ڪونه
هو ته تون ڪوڙي آهين،
تنهنجي قاتلن ڪپڙن تي
وشواس ڪيم،
تو ته ائين ڏيڪاري ڏنو
ته منهنجي شيوا ڪندينءَ

تو چيو تنهنجي ماءُ
اُٿڻ ۾ ماهر آهي
تون گهر ستو سنياليندي آهين،
ها، تو سچ چيو، منهنجو
گهر تو بهترين سنياليو!
تو تہ برباد ڪري ڇڏيو
جڏهن مون توکي راجا
جي ڪمري ۾ روئندو ڏنو
تڏهن مون اياٽيءَ ڪي
خبر ڪانہ هئي تہ تنهنجي
نظر راجا جي مندِيءَ تي آهي،
تو تہ وري ڪوڙ ڳالهائي،
نقلي ڳوڙها ڳاري ڇيو
تون پنهنجن سنن ڏينهن ڪي
ياد ڪري روئي رهي آهين
مان بي عقل هيس جو تو
تي پروسو ڪيم،
مون پاڻ سان پاڻ ئي
جٺ ڪئي ۽ تو ڪي
حد پار ڪرڻ جو موقعو ڏنو،
تو مون ڪي پنهنجي هيرن جي
هار جي ڳالهہ ٻڌائي،
تو مون ڪي هيرن جي هار
جي لالچ ڏني اُن

بدران مان تو کي پنهنجي راجا
سان هڪ رات گذارڻ جو شرط رکيو،
بس هڪ رات ....
توهان ٻنهي گڏجي چيو
بس هڪ رات ....
مان نادان
توکي پنهنجي پٽيار جي سيجا تي
سمهڻ ڏنم،
مون راجا کي منٿون
ڪيون ته تو کي قبول ڪري
صرف ڪجھ ڪلاڪن لاءِ قبول ڪري

مون ڀانيو ته اِها ڪا وڏي ڳالھ ناهي،
چو ته راجا جون ٻيون راڻيون به هيون،
مون کي پاڻ تي غرور ءِ
يقين هئو ته ڪا به چوڪري
مون ڪان راجا کي جدا نه ڪري سگھندي،
راجا جي زنان خاني ۾ ڪا به
عورت نه هئي جنهن جو ديدار
ڪري راجا مون کي وساري،
ڪيتريون ڪامڻيون آيون ويون،
مون کي ڪڍڻ به ڪنهن مان
خطرو ڪونه ٿيو،
پر تون.... تو ڇيهو رسايو،
ءِ مون کي ڏک ڏنو.

ڪؤنرُو

تون تہ پنهنجي پرينءَ جي ياڪُر

مِ سمائجي بي خوف ٿينءَ،

اِها غلطي ڪنهن بہ عورت

ڪي نہ ڪرڻ گهرجي،

تنهنجيءَ نادانيءَ ڪري

مون راجا ڪي ريجهايو،

تو تہ پنهنجيءَ شاديءَ ڪي

مذاق سمجهيو، ايڏو سستو بٽايو،

جو زيورن بدلي راجا ڏنو!

تو چا سوچيو تہ راجا ڪي

جڏهن خبر پوندي تہ هو رحمِ دل ٿيندو؟

ءَ تنهنجيءَ بيوقوفيءَ ڪي

معاف ڪندو؟

تنهنجي لالچ يلائي چِڏيندو؟

مون توڪي هڪ امولڪ هار ڏنو،

ءَ اُنهيءَ ذريعي تنهنجي

ور ءَ محل تي سوپ پاتي،

اِها جِڳھ پائڻ لاءِ مون

پاڻ پتوڙيو،

ءَ تو ڪي پتو بہ نہ پيو،

جيتوٽيڪ مان نوڪرياڻي ڪانہ هيس

مون پنهنجو محل چِڏيو

تنهنجي محل جو فرش ڈوتو،
مون کي ڄاڻ ٿئي تہ
هيءَ نماڻائي
منهنجي لاءِ سڀ در کوليندي،
هاڻي چنيسر فقط منهنجو آهي
ءَ تو کي قيمت چُڪائڻي آهي
اُميد تہ اِهي مڱيا
جيڪي تو تن تي سجايا
اِها مٽا سٽا صحيح آهي.

ليلا

هيءُ هيرن جو هار
منهنجي جيءَ جو جنجال
منهنجي پيڪي گهر ۾
جيڪي مون تي رشق کندا هئا،
اج اُهي ئي هلندي چلندي
مون کي زور سان مهٽا
ٿا ڏين،

تنهنجي رٿ شايد کامياب ٿي هوندي
پر مان پنهنجي پرينءَ کي پڪ پائيندس،
چو تہ اسان کئين گهٽا سال
گڏ گذاريا آهن،
هوُ ڄاڻي ٿو تہ مان

سندس هر ڳالهہ ء خيال
سمجهندي آهيان،
ء مون کي پڪ آهي تہ مان راجا
جي دل مان تنهنجو نالو
نشان مٽائيندس،
منهنجي چوٽ تي راجا جلد ئي
توکي وساريندو،

اُنهيء ڪاري رات
راجا کي نشي جي حالت ۾ آڻي
تون ء تنهنجي چالاڪ ماءُ
گڏجي سازش رچي ء
پنڊت گهرائي توهان شادي رچائي،
توهان هن کان زبردستي
اِنجام ورتو،

صبح جو راجا کي پنهنجيء
چُڪ جو احساس ٿيو
هوُ ڏاڍو پشيمان ٿيو
جڏهن هُن کي خبر پيئي
تہ تو کهڙي چال هلي آهي،
هوُ مون تي ڪاوڙيل هئو
پر هُن جي ناراضگي فقط
مون سان نہ هئي چو تہ تو

صرف مون کي نہ ٺگيو
پر اُن انسان سان بہ
دغابازي کئي جنهن کي تون
پيارڪندي آهين... اِهو کهڙو نينهن؟
جيتوٽيڪ اُن هڪ پل لاءِ
چنيسر تنهنجي حرکت قبول ڪئي
هو ضرور موٽي مون وٽ ايندو
چو تہ هوُ مون سان بيحد
محبت ڪندو آهي
ءِ تو ڪي هڪ ڏينهن
ضرور ڏڪاريندو.

ويچاري ليلا پنهنجو پرين
وڃايو،
پر پيار ۾ وفادار رهي
پاڻ پڇتايائين تہ هڪ پل
جي ڪمزوريءَ ڪري
پريتم رُسي ويو.
هڪ ڏينهن جاڪيرو
ليلا ڪان مدد گهرڻ آيو،
ليلا جي گُوٺ جي هڪ
سهٽيءَ تي جاڪيرو
فدا ٿيو هئو
شادي ڪرڻ پئي چاهيائين

اِنهيءَ ڪري ليلا ڪان سهارو وِٽ آيو،
ليلا چيس ته مان تنهنجي مدد
ضرور ڪندس پر منهنجي هڪ
شرط آهي،
جي تون چنيسر ڪي مون وٽ
وٺي ايندي ته مان
تنهنجي شادي اُنهيءَ حسين
نياٽيءَ سان ڪرائيندس.
جاڪيري جي شاديءَ ۾ چنيسر
سان گڏجڻ جي اِڇا ليلا
جي من ۾ اُٿي.
پوءِ جاڪيرو لڳي ويو راجا
ڪي مجائڻ ۾ ته
هُو سندس شاديءَ ۾ شامل ٿئي.
چنيسر جي مرضي ڪانه هئي
پر جاڪيري جو عرض ٻڌي
ڪيس ناڪاري نه سگهيو.
جاڪيري جي وهانءَ جي ڏينهن
پردي ۾ ويڪيل گائڪا
هڪ سوز ڀريو گيت
راجا جي سامهون پيش ڪيو،
راجا ٻي چئن ٽيو ۽
ڪيس پنهنجي پٽ راٺي ياد آئي
يادگرين جي طوفان ۾

راجا جون اکيون پرجي آيون،
هن سندريءَ جي کويل جيئان
مٺر آواز راجا جي کجھ
پيڙا دُور کئي،
راجا سندس گھونگھٽ کولڻ
جي خواهش کئي،
ليلا کي وري ڏسي وائڙو تيو.
اڄ ڏينهن تائين ليلا چنيسر
امرتا جي پاکر هِ
بڌل آهن،
جيئن تپت ۽ روشني
سانت هِ ساٿ رهندا آهن،
هڪ گھڙي بڌل خال هِ
چمکندڙ چپ جي اندر
قاتل ڌرتيءَ جي اندروني
حصي هِ،
ليلا نظر اچي ٿي،
ليلا پنهنجن لڙڪن مان
پاڻ هيرا رچي ٿي،
اِهي ئي سڀ کان املهہ آهن.

The Broken Bow

The Raja in his palace fine

to hear him did agree.

He mercifully called him in

and met him graciously.

Then prince and bard, one harmony,

one single 'self' became.

The Broken Bow

Beejal
The wind is quiet tonight, against
the crackling of the pyre.
There is no music sighing in the trees,
and my *surando*, which has been
my blessing and my curse,
hangs its peacock-crested head in shame.
What have I done, Sorath, that your King,
Rai Diyach of Junagadh, burns in this flame,
torso without a head?
So willingly he cut it off to pay my minstrel's fee,
though you, his distraught queen,
begged me to change my mind.
My bow still weeps, Sorath, at my misfortune
and the choice I had to make. I had no interest
in the salver full of jewels that King Annirai
gave my wife, but she promised that I would bring
Rai Diyach's head to him –
that my music would be enough
for Rai *saheb* to gladly agree.
I could have broken this promise that was made
on my behalf, but King Annirai would have
killed my family! Instead, when I brought
the precious head to him,
with my broken bow and burning hand,
he changed his mind and said I had done a great wrong,
killing a man so generous that
he would cut off his own head to pay a musician's debt.
It was for him that I had done this, yet he was right.

Sorath

Six nights we heard you, outside our palace walls.
Your plaintive notes took my husband to the gates
of ecstasy, and he invited you in to open the doors for him.
We all stopped to listen to the magic of your strings.
Even the birds outside were hushed upon the trees,
and you played on till my Rai Diyach flew to heaven
to meet the divinity that lay buried within himself,
and he returned to offer you diamonds and other gems.
You refused them all, Beejal; we thought you good,
until you stopped playing to make
your preposterous demand.
When my husband killed himself for you,
he murdered us all – the many queens who loved him,
and I learned to love him too, beyond myself.

I was to be King Annirai's bride, but Rai Diyach
would have none of it; he forced
my wedding procession to stop
in Junagadh, insisted I was too beautiful to belong
to anyone but him. And Ratno, the dear man
who brought me up, the only father I knew
amidst his clays and pots –
he had no choice but to give me up to him.
In doing this, Rai Diyach saved me,
for though neither of us knew it then,
King Annirai was my father and had cast me out,
the sixty-first daughter born to him,
and the river brought me to Ratno's loving arms.

Beejal

We must have met as infants on the rolling waves,
for your journey, and mine, are similar.

I, too, was cast out, though I was a wanted child,
a miracle for my mother, Rai Diyach's sister,
but I came with a prophecy –
that I would be born to her but would
grow up to kill the King.
She rejoiced at my birth
but the saint who gave the dire warning,
reminded her of the evil deed I was born to do,
so she steeled herself and set me afloat
to take me where the currents would.
It was the shepherd Damo who found me on the riverbank;
he took me home, for I was the water's gift
and in Annirai's kingdom, I spent many sweet hours
playing my *surando* as I watched the sheep.
The animals became my orchestra,
but sweetest of all were the notes of the deer
whose intestines lay gutted on a tree.
The wind plucked music from its dried-out strings
and the birds, enthralled, flew there to listen
to the sighing notes.
From this unfortunate creature, I learned
the best music comes from that silent space
that lives between the leaves,
and music for me became sorcery,
the magic that made my name.
But now, gracious Sorath, let me end
my journey as it began.
We started our lives on the water
and I must now join you in this fire.

Sorath
Your wife was greedy, and your King could not be trusted,
and while I cannot forgive you, I understand

no one can fight their destiny.
You destroyed my life, and yours as well.
The bow and strings are silenced.
Come, take my hand,
and let your *surando* sing again.

टुटलु कमानु

बीजल

हिन ऊंदाही राति में
चिखिया जे टड़िके में,
हवा ख़ामोशु आहे,
वण टिण पिणि सांति ऐं ग़मुगीनु आहिनि,
ऐं मुंहिंजो सुरीलो सुरंदो पिणु
जो मुंहिंजे लाइ सभाग़ो हुओ
अजु सिरापु थो महिसूसि थिए,
मोर पंख सां सींगारियलु सुरंदो
अजु शर्मसारु आहे,
सोरठ मूं छा कयो ?
जो जूनागढ़ जो राजा राइ ड़ियाचु अजु
हीअं बाहि जे भंभाट में
धड़ बिना सिरु ब़रे पियो,
हुन मूं जहिड़े मामूली जाजक जो
उजूरो चुकाइण लाइ
पंहिंजो सिरु ख़ुशीअ सां कपे ड़िनो,
तोड़े तो व्याकुलु राणीअ
मूंखे मिंथूं कयूं ऐं लीलायो
त मां मनु मटायां.
सोरठ मुंहिंजो कमानु मुंहिंजीअ बदिक़िस्मतीअ ते
अ़ज्ञा बि ज़ारो ज़ारि रोए पियो,
पर मां लाचारु होसि,
मूंखे राजा अनीराइ जे ड़िनल
हीरनि जवाहरनि सां भरियल थाल में

का बि दिलचस्पी न हुई,
उहे माल त मुंहिंजीअ
ज़ाल क़बूलु कया
मूंखां इन्जामु वरिताई त
मां राजा राइ ड़ियाच जो सिरु वढे ईंदुसि
मुंहिंजो संगीतु सग़ारो आहे
राजा राइ ड़ियाच खे मोहे मआइण लाए,
मां पंहिंजो इहो वचनु ज़रूर
टोड़े सघां हा.
पर राजा अनीराइ मुंहिंजे सज़े
कुटंब खे मारे छड़े हा !
जड़िहं मूं राजा राइ ड़ियाच जो
सिरु वञी अनीराइ खे ड़िनो
पंहिंजे टुटल कमान ऐं ब़रंदड़ हथनि सां,
अनीराइ यकिदमु नाकारी थियो
मूं खे गुनहगारु सड़ियो,
ड़ोरापो ड़िनाईं त मूं अहिड़े
फ़राख़दिलि राजा जो क़तलु कयो
जंहिं सिरु क़ुर्बानु कयो सुर ते
हिक साज़ींदड़ जो क़र्जु अदा करण लाए,
मूं त इहो बुछिड़ो कमु
अनीराइ जे हुकम ते ई कयो
त बि हू सही हो.

सोरठ
छह रातियूं लग़ातारु महल
जे भितियुनि जे ब़ाहिरां
असां तुंहिंजे सुरंदे जो

सुरीलो आवाजु बुधो,
तुंहिंजनि दिलिसोजु सुरनि
मुंहिंजे भतार खे मस्तीअ
में बे ख़ुदि कयो,
राजा तोखे महल जे
अंदरि अचण जी नींड ड़िनी
जीअं तूं पंहिंजे संगीत सां
राजा जे रूह जा दर खोलीं
असां सभु तुंहिंजीअ तंदु तंवार
जे जादूअ में लीनु थियासीं,
पखियुनि जूं लातियूं पिण
सुरंदे जे सोज़ में सांति थियूं,
तूं चंगु चोरींदो रहें
जेसिताईं राजा सुरनि जे मौज में
ख़्याली सुर्ग ताईं उड़ामियो
उन्हीअ ख़ुदाईअ खे ग़ोल्हे लधाईं
जेका संदसि रूह में भरियल हुई

मोटी राजा राइ ड़ियाच
तो खे हीरा, मोती, नगीना इनामु आछा,
पर तो त उहे सभु नाकारिया
असां तुंहिंजीअ ईमानदारीअ जी साराह कई,
पर असां अण ज़ाणु
असां तुंहिंजो मतिलबु न समझो
उहो त बेमानाइतो ऐं बेहूदो निकितो
राजा तुंहिंजे सुरनि ते
पंहिंजी जानि क़ुर्बानु कई

पाण सां गडु राजा असां सभिनी
राणियुनि खे जेके खेसि बेहदि भाईंदियूं हुयूं
तिनि खे तो जीअरे मारे छड़ियो,

मां पाण खां वधीक
राजा खे प्यारु करणु सिखियसि.
मुंहिंजो विहाऊं त राजा अनीराइ
सां थियणो हो
पर राजा राइ डियाच मुंहिंजी
ज़ञ ज़बर्दस्ती रोके,
हकुमु हलायाई
मुंहिंजे सूहं जो हक़दारु फ़क़्तु हू पाण आहे,
ऐं मुंहिंजो पीउ रतिनो जंहिं
मूंखे चीकी मिटीअ ऐं
घड़नि जे विच में पालियो,
संदसि मर्ज़ी कान हली हुई
मुंहिंजो हथु राजा राइ डियाच जे
हथ में ड़िनाई,

दरअसलु राजा राइ डियाच
मूंखे बचायो हो,
छो त तड़हिं असां मां
कंहिं खे बि ख़बर कान हुई
त राजा अनीराइ हक़ीक़त में मुंहिंजो पीउ हो,
मां हिन जे सठि धीउरनि में
वाधि हुयसि,
हिन मूंखे संदूक़ में पूरे
दरियाह में वाहे छड़ियो,

रतने मूंखे किनारे ते लधो
प्यार सां पाले, वड्डो कयो.

बीजल
असां ज़रूरि नंढिपिणि में
उछलंदड़ छोलियुनि में
गड़िया हूंदासीं,
तुंहिंजो ऐं मुंहिंजो
सफ़रु हिक जहिड़ो,
मूंखे पिणु संदूक़ में
बंदि करे सरनि दरियाह कयो वियो,
तोड़े मां हिक फ़क़ीर जे
दुआउनि सां ज़ावलु पुटु होसि
मुंहिंजी माउ जा राइ ड्रियाच
जी भेण हुई उन लाइ हिकु
चमत्कारी ब्रारु होसि,
पर मुंहिंजे जन्म सां गड़ोगड़ु
आई हिक अजीबु अग़कथी
त मां वड्डो थी राजा राइ ड्रियाच
जो क़तलु कंदुसि
मुंहिंजे ज़मण ते माउ ड्राढी
ख़ुशु हुई,
पर जंहिं ज्योतिषीअ धधिको ड्रींदड़
अहिड़ी अग़कथी कई
त मां
बुछिड़ो कारनामो करण लाए
पैदा थियो आहियां,

उन वक़्तु मुंहिंजीअ माउ पंहिंजे दिलि
ते पथरु रखियो,
ऐं मूंखे दरियाह में लोड़िहियो वियो
मां सीर जे तेजु वहिकरे
सां वञी किनारे पहुतुसि,
जिति हिक रेढार मूंखे लधो,
मूंखे अपिनायो
छो त मां संदसि लाए वरुण देव
जो वरदानु होसि
अनीराइ जे राज़ में कईं वरिह्न
ख़ुशीअ में गुज़ारिया,
मां पंहिंजीअ मस्तीअ में लीनु
सुरंदो वज़ाइंदो होसि
रिढूं चारींदो होसि
उहे जानवर मुंहिंजा साथी थिया,
ऐं मुंहिंजा गीत बुधंदा रहिया,
पर सभ खां सोज़ भरियो सुरु
शिकारु थियल हिरण जे
आंडनि मां निकितो
जेके वण ते टंगियल हुआ,
हवा संगीत जूं धुनूं
सुकल तंदुनि मां कढियूं
पखी, मोहिति थी उड़ामी
उहे सूसाट वारा सुर बुधण लगा,
उन्हीअ बदिनसीब हिरण खां
मां सिखियुसि त सभिनी खां
आला संगीतु उभिरे थो
सावनि पतनि जे विच जे

ख़ामोशु ख़ाल मां,
संगीत मुंहिंजे लाए रूह जो खाजु बणियो,
उहो जादू जंहिं सां मां मशहूरु थियुसि,
पर हाणे अभागी़ सोरठ! मां पंहिंजो
सफ़रु पूरो कयां जीअं शुरु कयो
असां जीवनु शुरु कयो निर्मल जल मां,
हाणे मां अन्त में तोसां
हिन आगि में जुड़ंदुसि

सोरठ
तुंहिंजी ज़ाल ड्राढी लालची हुई,
तुंहिंजे राजा अनीराइ ते
को न भर्वसो हो,
मां तोखे हर्गिज़ि माफु
न कंदुसि,
मां समझां थी त कर्म जो लिखियो
केरु न चुकाए न सघंदो,
तो मुंहिंजी ज़िंदगी तबाह कई
ऐं पंहिंजी पिणि,

कमान ऐं तंदूं सदाईं लाइ
ख़ामोशु थियूं
अचु, मुंहिंजो हथु झलु,

ऐं पंहिंजे सुरंदे खे
वरी वज़णु ड्रे... वरी तंदूं तंवार.

نتل كمان

پيجل

هن اونداهي رات ۾
چكيا جي تڙكي ۾
هوا خاموش آهي،
وٽ نٽ سانت ۽ غمگين آهن،
۽ منهنجو سُريلو سرندو پٽ
جو منهنجي لاءِ سياڳو هئو
اڄ تہ سراپ تو محسوس ٿئي،
مور پنک سان سينگاريل سرندو
اڄ شرمسار آهي،
سورٺ! مون چا كيو؟
جو جوناڳڙھ جو راجا راءِ ڏياچ اڄ
هيئن باھ جي پنيات ۾
ڏڙ بنا سِر ٻري پيو،
هُن مون جهڙي معامولي جاجک
أجورو چكائڻ لاءِ
پنهنجو سِر خوشيءَ سان كپي ڏنو،
توڙي تو وياكُل راٽيءَ
مون كي منٿون كيون ۽ ليلايو
تہ مان من مٽايان،
سورٺ! منهنجو كمان منهنجيءَ بدقسمتيءَ تي
اڄا بہ زارو زار روئي پيو،

پر مان لاچار هوس،

مون کي راجا انيراءِ جي ڏنل

هيرن جواهرن سان پريل ٿال ۾

کابہ دلچسپي نہ هئي،

اُهي مال تہ منهنجيءَ

زال قبول کيا

ءِ مون کان انجام ورتائين تہ

مان راجا راءِ ڏياچ جو سِر وِڍي ايندس

منهنجو سنگيت سِجارو آهي

راجا راءِ ڏياچ کي موهي مجائڻ لاءِ،

مان پنهنجو اِهو وچن ضرور

توڙي سگهان ها،

پر راجا انيراءِ منهنجي سجي

کَٽنب کي ماري چڏي ها!

جڏهن مون راجا راءِ ڏياچ جو

سِر وڍي انيراءِ کي ڏنو

پنهنجي ٽِٽل کمان ءِ هرندڙ هٿن سان،

انيراءِ يڪدم ناکاري ٿي

مون کي گنهگار سڏيو،

ڏوراپو ڏنائين تہ مون اهڙي

فراخدل راجا جو قتل کيو

جنهن سِر قربان کيو سُر تي

هڪ سازيندڙ جو قرض ادا کرڻ لاءِ،

مون تہ اِهو بچڙو کم

انيراءِ جي حڪم تي ئي ڪيو
ته ٻہ جي هوُ صحيح هو.

سورٺ

ڇهہ راتيون لڳاتار محل
جي يتين جي ٻاهران
اسان تنهنجي سرندي جو
سُريلو آواز ٻڌو،
تنهنجن دلسوز سُرن
منهنجي ٻتار ڪي مستيءَ
مِ بيخود ڪيو،
راجا تو ڪي محل جي
اندر اچڻ جي نيند ڊني
جيئن تون پنهنجي سنگيت سان
راجا جي روح جا در ڪولين
اسان سڀ تنهنجيءَ تند تنوار
جي جادوءَ مِ لين ٿياسين،
پڪين جونلاتيون ٻڌ
سُرندي جي سوز مِ سانت ٿي،
ءَ تون چنگ رهئين چوريندو
جيستائين راجا سُرن جي موج مِ
خيالي سُرڳ تائين اڏاميو
اُنهيءَ خدائيءَ ڪي ڳولهي لڌائين
جيڪا سندس روح مِ پريل هئي

موتي راجا راجا راءِ ڏياچ

توکي هيرا، موتي، نگينا اِنعام آڇا،

پر تو تہ اُهي سڀ ناکاريا

اسان تنهنجيءَ ايمانداريءَ جي ساراھ کئي،

پر اسان اڏ جاڏ

اسان تنهنجو مطلب نہ سمجهو

اُهو تہ بي معنائتو ۽ بيهودو نکتو

راجا تنهنجي سُرن تي

پنهنجي جان قربان کئي

پاڏ سان گڏ راجا اسان سيني

راڻين کي جيڪي کيس بيحد پائينديون هيون

تن کي تو جيئري ماري ڇڏيو،

مان پاڏ کان وڏيک

راجا کي پيار کرڻ سکيس.

منهنجو وهانءُ تہ راجا انيراءِ

سان ٿيڻو هو

پر راجا راءِ ڏياچ منهنجي

جيج زبردستي روکي،

حکر هلايائين

منهنجي سونهنجو حقدار فقط هوُ پاڏ آهي،

۽ منهنجو پيءُ رتنو جنهن

مون کي چيڪي مڻيءَ ۽

گهڙن جي وچ ۾ پاليو،

سندس مرضي ڪانہ هلي
منهنجو هت راجا راءِ ڏياچ جي
هت ۾ ڏنائين،
دراصل راجا راءِ ڏياچ
مون ڪي بچايو هو،
چو ت تنڌن اسان مان
ڪنهن ڪي بہ خبر ڪانہ هئي
تہ راجا انيراءِ حقيقت ۾ منهنجو پيءُ هو،
مان هن جي ست ڏيئرن ۾
واڌ هيس،
هن مون ڪي صندوق ۾ پوري
درياه ۾ وهائي ڇڏيو،
رتني مون ڪي ڪناري تي لڌو
پيار سان پالي، وڏو ڪيو.

پيجل

اسان ضرور نندیپٽ ۾
اُڃلندڙ چولين ۾
گڏیا هونداسين،
تنهنجو ۽ منهنجو
سفر هڪ جهڙو،
مون ڪي پٽ صندوق ۾
بند ڪري سرن درياه ڪيو ويو،
توڙي مان هڪ فقير جي

دعائن سان چاول پٽ هوس
منهنجي ماءُ جا راءِ ڏياچ
جي پيٽ هئي لاءِ هڪ
چمتڪاري ٻار هوس،
پر منهنجي جنم سان گڏوگڏ
آئي هڪ عجيب اڳڪٿي
تہ مان وڏو ٿي راجا راءِ ڏياچ
جو قتل ڪندس
منهنجي ڄمڻ تي ماءُ ڏاڍي
خوش هئي،
پر جنهن جيوتشيءَ اهڙو ڏڏڪو ڏيندڙ
اهڙي اڳڪٿي ڪئي
تہ مان
بچيڙو ڪارنامو ڪرڻ لاءِ
پيئدا ٿيو آهيان،
اُن وقت منهنجيءَ ماءُ پنهنجي دل
تي پٿر رکيو،
۽ مون کي درياھ ۾ لوڙهيو ويو
مان سير جي تيز وهڪري
سان وڃي ڪناري تي پھتس،
جت هڪ رِيڍار مون کي لڌو،
مون کي اپنايو
جو تہ مان سندس لاءِ وروٽ ديو
جو وردان هوس

انيراءُ جي راڄ ۾ ڪئين ورهيه
خوشيءَ ۾ گذاريا،
مان پنهنجيءَ مستيءَ ۾ لِين
سُرندو وڄائيندو هوس
ريون چاريندو هوس
اِهي جانور منهنجا ساٿي ٿيا،
ءَ منهنجا گيت ٻڌندا رهيا،
پر سپ کان سوز ڀريو سُر
شڪار ٿيل هرڻ جي
آنڊن مان نڪتو
جيڪي وڻ تي ٽنگيل هئا،
هوا سنگيت جون ڌنون
سڪل تندن مان ڪڍيون
ءَ پڪي، موهت ٿي أڏامي
أھي سوساٽ وارا سُر ٻڌڻ لڳا،
اِنهيءَ بدنصيب هرڻ ڪان
مان سڪيس ته سيني ڪان
اعليٰ سنگيت أُيري ٿو
ساون پتن جي وچ جي
خاموش خال مان،
سنگيت منهنجي لاءِ روح جو خاڄ ٿيو،
أهو جادو جنهن سان مان مشهور ٿيس،
پر هاڻي اياڳي سورٽ! مان پنهنجو
سفر پورو ڪيان جيئن شروع ڪيو

اسان جيون شروع ڪيو نرمل جل مان،
هاڻي مان انت مِ توسان
هن آگ مِ جڙندس

سورت

تنهنجي زال ڏاڍي لالچي هئي،
تنهنجي راجا انيراءَ تي
ڪو نَ يروسو هو،
مان توکي هرگز معاف
نَ ڪندس،
مان سمجهان ٿي تہ ڪرم جو لکيو
ڪير بہ چڪائي نَ سگهندو،
تو منهنجي زندگي تباه ڪئي
۽ پنهنجي پڻ،

ڪمان ۽ تندون سدائين لاءِ
تائين خاموش ٿيون
اڄ، منهنجو هٿ جهل،

۽ پنهنجي سُرندي ڪي
وري وڄٽ ڏي.... وري تند تنوار.

Appendix

Cover
The cover depicts a *surando*, a traditional Sindhi folk instrument.

Foreword
Mohan Gehani is a noted Sindhi scholar, playwright, translator and poet. Born in Karachi, Sind, on January 20, 1938, he belongs to the select community of Sindhi writers who lived through the Partition of India. His numerous awards include the Saeen G M Syed memorial award at the World Sindhi Congress in London in 2005, and the Sahitya Akademi award in 2011. He has also received awards from the National Council for the Promotion of Sindhi Language; the lifetime achievement award from Akhil Bharat Sindhi Boli ain Sahit Sabha and a translation award by Sahitya Akademi in 2016. He was a member of the Sindhi advisory board for Sahitya Akademi from 2007 to 2012. Read all his writing here: *https://mohangehani.com*

'Sind'(from the Perso-Arabic سنڌ), as referred to here and elsewhere in the book, is now spelled as 'Sindh'. Since the references in this book are to its original identity, the earlier spelling has been retained. The term 'Sind' was discontinued in 1988 after an amendment passed in the Sindh Assembly.

Author's Note
Read more about Jhulelal here: *https://www.jhulelal.com/completestory.htm*

The Sindhu Roars

♦ Indus river was known to ancient Indians in Sanskrit as the Sindhu and to the Persians as Hindu. The Greeks called it the *Indós* and the Romans referred to it as *Indus*. The name India is derived from Indus.

♦ C. A. Kincaid writes in his book, *Folk Tales of Sind and Guzarat* (1925): "The beauties of Sind are not for the stranger, or casual visitor. He, perhaps merely seeking the shortest and quickest route to some temporary post up North, or possibly to his permanent home in the damp, grey West, notices only torrid heat, arid wastes, blinding glare, suffocating dust and a coastal Port somewhat reminiscent of Suez or Port Said. Not for him the enchanting views from the little islands at Bhukkar, or from the banks of the lower reaches of the Indus below Hyderabad. Not for him the green grain fields and shady forests that fringe the great river between Larkana and the late Capital. Not for him the scent of the old Kumbar Road, or the myriad bird life of the Munchar Lake. Not for him the moonlight on the great desert on our Eastern frontier; or the sunrise from the Indus delta, throwing its golden shafts across Karachi's beautiful lagoon to the rugged skyline of the Hub hills... But for the old Sindhi these things mean much."

♦ Munchar (also known as Manchar) Lake, located west of the Indus River, in the Jamshoro and Dadu districts of Sindh, is the largest freshwater lake in Pakistan and one of the largest lakes in Asia.

- The Sarasvati River is an ancient river, mythologised and first mentioned in the Rigveda. The lost river is believed to have flown independently of the Indus into the Arabian Sea, perhaps along the courses of now-defunct rivers such as the Ghaggar, Hakra and Nara. Read more about it here: *https://www.nature.com/articles/s41598-017-05745-8*

- Palla – The nomadic *palla* fish travels from the sea to the Indus River between May and August, feeding from the silt of the river and sea. This creates a unique flavour that cannot be replicated in farmed fish. The fish is meaty, has sharp bones and is rich in omega-three fatty acids. The *palla* also has a spiritual significance for Sindh. Learn more about it here: *https://artsandculture.google.com/story/palla-fish-from-the-indus-river-in-sindh-soch/IgWBnPTyFHyIIg?hl=en*

- The word Sind is a Persian derivative of Sindhu, a Sanskrit term meaning 'river'. It has been influenced by many cultures and conquerors. The Greeks, under the command of Alexander the Great, conquered Sind in 325 BC. This land, the first in the subcontinent to come under Islamic rule, saw many ups and downs through the Achaemenid Era (516-326 BC), the Hellenistic era (326–317 BC), Mauryan Era (316–180 BC), Indo-Greek era (180–90 BC), Indo Scythians (90–20 BC), Gupta Empire (345-455 AD), Sassanian

Empire (325–489 AD), Rai Dynasty (c. 489 – 632 AD), Brahmin dynasty (c.632 – c.724 AD), among others.

In the Medieval era (711-854 A.D.), the Arab expansion towards the east reached the Sind region beyond Persia. Later, Sind was ruled by the Habbari Arab dynasty (854–1024), marking the end of direct rule by the Umayyad and Abbasid Caliphates. The Habbaris were defeated by the Turkic Sultan Mahmud Ghaznavi. Sind was also ruled by the Soomra dynasty (1011–1333), a local Sindhi Muslim dynasty, the Samma dynasty (1333–1520) and the Arghuns (1520–1591). In the early modern age, Sind was brought into the Mughal Empire by Akbar, who was born in Umerkhot in Sind. Later, it came under the Kalhora dynasty (1701–1783), the Talpur dynasty (1783–1843) and then under British Rule from 1843–1947.

Mohan Gehani's *History of Sindh* may be downloaded for free from his website: *https://mohangehani.com/history/history-of-sindh-by-mohan-gehani/*

♦ The story goes that the great saint Lal Shahbaz, born in A. H. 538, once wanted to travel to an island in the Persian Gulf to make the fakir Sheikh Jalal his disciple. No boats were available, so Lal Shahbaz threw his 'kishta' or begging bowl into the water, and it became a boat (C.A. Kincaid,

Folk Tales of Sind and Guzarat, The Daily Gazette Press Ltd., Karachi, 1925, pg 8)

The quotes at the beginning of each story are sourced from *Shah-jo-Risalo*, translated into English by Elsa Kazi (Elsa Gertrude Loesch). Born in 1884, the German poet and painter married the Sindhi scholar Allama Kazi in 1910. She died in 1967 and is remembered with the epithet, 'Mother Elsa'. (*https://apnaorg.com/books/english/shah-jo-risalo/book.php?fldr=book*)

Call of the Mountains: SASUI-PUNHOON

This is the story of a young woman who is set afloat in a canal as a baby after a priest declares she is destined to marry someone from another community. Mohammed, the chief of a washerman's clan, adopts her, and she grows up to be a beautiful young woman named Sasui, named after the moon. Tales of her beauty reach the ears of Punhoon, the prince of Kech Makran, who arrives in the garb of a trader. The two fall in love, and after initial objections, Mohammed agrees to the match on condition that Punhoon stays back and becomes a washerman. Punhoon's brothers, however, abduct the young man and take him home. A distraught Sasui sets off on treacherous terrain to find Punhoon, only to meet an evil shepherd who tries to take advantage of her. Sasui prays for safety, and the ground opens up to swallow her. Meanwhile, Punhoon returns for Sasui and sees a sliver of her garment peeping up from the ground. He prays to be united with her, and the ground swallows him, too. This story is seen as an allegory depicting the unity of the Self with the Divine.

Karvaan: Caravan

The Fire Within: SOHINI-MEHAR

Another story of star-crossed lovers is that of Sohini-Mehar. Sohini ('Beautiful'), the daughter of a wealthy potter, falls in love with Izzat Beg, the son of a rich businessman in Turkistan named Mirza Ali. Izzat, blinded by his love for Sohini, loses his fortune and ends up in the employ of the potter, becoming 'Mehar', herder of buffaloes. When Sohini is forcibly married to Damma, a heartbroken Mehar disappears into the jungles to join a group of sadhus and settles as a Jogi on the bank opposite Sohini's home. His fame as a holy man spreads. One day, Sohini comes to meet the holy man and recognises his true identity. The lovers reunite; Mehar crosses the river every night to visit her, bringing a fish for them to enjoy. One night, however, when no fish is available, Mehar cuts off a piece of his own leg to feed Sohini. She is horrified to learn the truth and decides that Mehar, in his weakened state, must not cross the river to meet her; she must go to him instead. Sohini swims across every night with the help of a pitcher and does so even when the river is in spate. On a particularly stormy night, Sohini ignores all warnings and plunges into the water, not realising that her suspicious sister-in-law has replaced the pitcher with one of unbaked clay. Sohini, realising her life is in danger, calls out to Mehar in distress. He jumps into the river to save his beloved Sohini but, with his injured leg, is unable to meet the force of the waves. Both go down, embracing each other in the water for eternity.

Magarmacch: Crocodiles
Sattvic: This suggests a serene, harmonious state of mind.
Odhni: A garment used by women to cover the upper part of their bodies and their heads.
Martbans are jars for pickles or sauces and *chatis* are globular pots. Read more about them here: *https:// www.harappa.com/excavations/1921/earthenware-martban-and-two-lotas*. A *surahi* is also a traditional Indian earthenware pot used to store water.

Princess of Illusion: MOOMAL-RANO

In 16th-century Sukkur, a Gujarat chieftain named Nand had nine daughters. Moomal was the most beautiful, and Soomal the most intelligent. Once, while on a hunt, the King encountered a swine whose magical front tooth could make the river recede; he killed it and used the tooth to bury his treasure where he believed no one could find it. A Jogi, however, tricked Moomal into parting with the tooth while the king was away and stole these riches. The angry king wished to kill his daughter, but Soomal came to her sister's rescue and promised their father she would recover the king's wealth. And so, Soomal built the Kak palace in Jaisalmer – an enchanted castle designed to entrap the many suitors who arrived there for Moomal's hand.

Only one suitor, Rano of Umarkot, proved worthy of her, but their love was ill-fated. Hamir Soomro,

Umarkot's jealous ruler, imprisoned Rano, freeing him only on the condition that he would no longer visit Moomal. Rano agreed, but broke the promise, travelling to Jaisalmer every night and returning at dawn. When he was imprisoned again, and unable to visit his lover, a devastated and bewildered Moomal asked her sister to dress like Rano and keep her company. One night, when Rano could get away, he was furious to discover that there was someone else in Moomal's bed. Moomal tried to convince him of her fidelity but eventually travelled to Umarkot disguised as a rich merchant in an effort to befriend Rano. As they played a game of chess, Rano realised it was Moomal, but he still refused to accept her. In despair, Moomal burned herself on a pyre. A distraught Rano, now convinced of her love, followed her into the flames and in death, the lovers were united forever.

The Keenjhar's Song: NOORI-JAM TAMACHI

In the fourteenth century, when Jaam Tamachi of the Samma dynasty was the ruler of Sind in Thatta, he fell in love with Noori, a girl from a fisherfolk community near the Keenjhar lake. He brought her to the palace as his bride and showered her with unimaginable luxuries, in the process completely ignoring all his other wives who did everything they could to gain the king's attention. Noori, however, hankered for her humble origins, shunning all ornaments and dressing in simple clothes. The king, charmed by her simplicity, declared her his reigning queen. To this day, Noori is considered a symbol of humility, and the story is interpreted as an example of how the Master will seek out those who are true to themselves and yet remain humble. Sadhu T.L. Vaswani (1879 –1966) was inspired by this and adopted 'Noori' as his pen name. Noori is said to be buried in the middle of Keenjhar Lake, and the shrine here is, to this day, a popular tourist attraction.

The Flute and the Tree: MARUI-UMAR

This is the story of Marui, a peasant woman who remains steadfast to her land and her people even though she spends years in captivity after Umar Soomro, the ruler of Umarkot, abducts her. Umar tries everything to get her to yield – entreaties, threats, promises to make her the reigning queen, and much more. Marui, however, continues to wear rags; she insists that she must go back to her village Maleer and to the man she is to marry. Then, one day, Umar realises that Marui's mother had once been his wet nurse and Marui is, therefore, like a sister to him. Struck with remorse, he takes her home. Her people, however, refuse to accept her because they believe she has lost her virtue to the king. Marui has to prove her chastity by holding a hot rod and emerges unscathed; Umar Soomro, too, passes the same test. For the Sindhi community, Marui has come to symbolise patriotism and a return to one's roots.

Diamonds and Coal: LEELA-CHANESAR

This is the story of Queen Leela, who lost her King Chanesar because she was tempted by greed, in the shape of a diamond necklace worth ₹9 lakh. Kounru, the daughter of the ruler Khangar in Lakhpat, Kutch, has fallen in love with King Chanesar and decides to entice him away from his bride. She arrives at Chanesar and Leela's palace in Devalkot with her mother Murki, and with the help of the King's minister, Jakhro, the two women enter the palace in the guise of servants. The unsuspecting Leela asks Kounru to clean the king's private bedchamber – a task that Kounru finds painful, being so close and yet so far from the man she loves. Leela finds her weeping one day and asks what is wrong; Kounru tells her that she, too, was once a princess and had costly ornaments, including a diamond necklace that could banish darkness itself. Leela sees the necklace and is dazzled. She agrees to a deal that Kounru offers – the jewellery in exchange for a night with the king. Leela agrees, only to find that Kounru's mother has arranged for a priest, and that Kounru has married Chanesar, who is in a drunken stupor. When the king realises what Leela has done, he is furious and banishes her from his kingdom. Leela realises her folly and repents but Chanesar is adamant; he refuses to take her back. Many years later, though the king has forgotten her, Leela takes Jakhro's help to meet the king again, disguised as a veiled singer. The king, struck by the sweetness of her voice, commands her to remove her veil. When he sees her, the long-dormant love is rekindled. The story ends with both Chanesar and Leela falling into a swoon together, their love immortalised forever.

Though the story is known as that of Leela and Chanesar, the poem in this book is a conversation between the two women, Leela and Kounru.

Nau lakh haar: ₹9 lakh necklace
Koyla: Coal

The Broken Bow: SORATH-RAI DIYACH

Once upon a time in Junagadh, Rai Khangar – also known as Rai Diyach because he was a giver – had a sister who desperately wanted a baby. When, after many prayers, she was finally granted a son, her joy dimmed as a saint told her this baby was destined to kill her brother. So, despite her grief, the woman cast her baby into the river, to float away in a basket towards his destiny. The basket reached the kingdom of King Annirai, where a shepherd named Damo found the baby and brought him up as his own son, naming him Beejal – 'water's gift'. Beejal grew up to become famous for his musical prowess, even fashioning a stringed instrument from the dried-out intestines of a deer in the forest.

King Annirai, meanwhile, had also cast out his own daughter into the arms of the river; he had already fathered sixty girls, and one more was certainly unwanted. The child, Sorath, grew up in Rai Diyach's kingdom in the home of Ratno the potter. When Annirai heard of Sorath's beauty, he decided to marry her, not realising it was his own daughter he was trying to wed. Rai Diyach would have none of it. He felt that a king from another region had no right to marry the girl; as the ruler, this privilege belonged to him. Rai Diyach, therefore, forcibly married Sorath, and proved to be a good husband to her.

An angry Annirai attacked Junagadh and was repulsed. Smarting under the humiliation, he offered a plate of jewels to whoever would bring him Rai Diyach's head. Beejal's wife took the jewels, telling the king that her husband would carry out the deed. Beejal refused.

However, when he realised that King Annirai would wipe out his family for failing to perform the task, he reluctantly agreed, and visited the palace at Junagadh, where he played his melodious tunes. Rai Diyach, entranced by the music, invited him in and offered anything that he wanted in return. To Sorath's horror, Beejal demanded her husband Diyach's head and the king readily agreed. Beejal returned to King Annirai with Diyach's head in a bag, only to find that Annirai had changed his mind. Annirai, who accused him of being greedy, banished him from the kingdom, and Beejal, filled with remorse, rushed back to Junagadh, where he found Sorath about to commit sati at Rai Diyach's funeral pyre. Beejal decided to join her and pay for the dark deed he committed with his life.

In this complex and tragic tale, all three perish – Rai Diyach, Sorath and Beejal – while Beejal's wife realises the price she has had to pay for her avarice.

The Author

MENKA SHIVDASANI

Menka Shivdasani, a Mumbai-based poet, editor and translator, is the author of four previous poetry collections. She is co-translator of *Freedom and Fissures*, an anthology of Sindhi Partition poetry (Sahitya Akademi, 1998), and editor of *If the Roof Leaks, Let it Leak*, an anthology of women's writing for Sound and Picture Archives for Research on Women (2014). She has also edited *The BigBridge Book of Contemporary Indian Poetry* (2024), originally published as online anthologies for the American ezine in 2013 and 2015. Menka has collaborated with the senior Sindhi poet Mohan Gehani on three of his poetry collections in English translation. Her awards include the Ethos Literary Award (2019) and the inaugural WE Eunice de Souza Award (2020).

Menka co-founded Poetry Circle in Bombay in 1986 and has organised poetry festivals for 100 Thousand Poets for Change since 2011. She is Co-Chair, Asia Pacific Writers and Translators (APWT). Her work as a journalist includes 18 books, co-authored/edited with Raju Kane, three of which were released by the then Indian Prime Minister Atal Bihari Vajpayee.

The Translator

BARKHA KHUSHALANI

Barkha Khushalani is a poet, film-maker, columnist, lyricist, and translator. She received the NCPSL award for translating Sudha Murty's book, *The Day I Stopped Drinking Milk,* into Sindhi. Maharashtra Rajya Sindhi Sahitya Academy awarded her for her book on children's poems *Dadi Thi Vanee*. She writes in three languages – Sindhi, Hindi and English.

She has written the screenplay, dialogue, and lyrics of two songs in the Sindhi feature film with English subtitles *Aakhreen Train...The Last Train*, which was released in 2023. She is also one of the four producers of the film, which is based on a love story during the Partition penned by her father, Thakur Chawla. This film is a humble endeavour to promote the Sindhi language through cinema. It has been appreciated in cities all over India.

BLACK EAGLE BOOKS

www.blackeaglebooks.org
info@blackeaglebooks.org

Black Eagle Books, an independent publisher, was founded as a nonprofit organization in April, 2019. It is our mission to connect and engage the Indian diaspora and the world at large with the best of works of world literature published on a collaborative platform, with special emphasis on foregrounding Contemporary Classics and New Writing.